KT-152-689

Please return/renew this item by the last date shown on this label, or on your self-service receipt.

To renew this item, visit **www.librarieswest.org.uk** or contact your library.

Your Borrower Number and PIN are required.

LibrariesWest

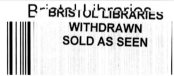

Also by Polly Ho-Yen and published by Corgi Books:

Boy in the Tower

WHERE MONSTERS LIE

POLLY HO-YEN

CORGI

For my sister, Hanna

CORGI BOOKS

UK | USA | Canada | Ireland | Australia
India | New Zealand | South Africa

Corgi Books is part of the Penguin Random House group of companies
whose addresses can be found at global.penguinrandomhouse.com.

www.penguin.co.uk
www.puffin.co.uk
www.ladybird.co.uk

Penguin
Random House
UK

First published 2016

001

Text copyright © Polly Ho-Yen, 2016

The moral right of the author has been asserted

Typeset in 11.5/15.5 pt ITC New Baskerville Std
Jouve (UK), Milton Keynes
Printed in Great Britain by Clays Ltd, St Ives plc

A CIP catalogue record for this book is available from the British Library

ISBN: 978–0–552–56917–0

All correspondence to:
Corgi Books
Penguin Random House Children's
80 Strand, London WC2R 0RL

The loch looked black today. Blacker than it ever has. As dark and black as the sky at night, but it was daytime. It was daytime.

I felt as if I was being drawn to it. I had to see it – I wanted to, or needed to. Or both. I had to see the water for myself.

It's as though, if I don't keep my eye on it, it might rise up. It would engulf me, sink me. If I keep my eye on it, I feel safe.

But what do I do when I fall asleep?

Chapter One

It began on the night of the offering. The night Buster disappeared.

Buster's my rabbit. Or he was, anyway.

It was dark that night. The kind of darkness that becomes one with the cold. It crept around our necks, biting at our toes like something living. Though I knew the loch lay before us, I couldn't see it. All I could see in front of me was blackness.

I was with Finn and all the other kids in the village. We were crowded around Old Bill, one of the oldies, who held the food parcel high above our heads with one hand while we chanted at him to '*Throw it, throw it, throw it!*'

Just as Old Bill lobbed the package, wrapped up in string like a present, high, effortlessly, into the air, I heard Mum behind me.

'Effie! Careful! Stand back!'

I wasn't even standing that close to the edge, but Mum pulled me backwards behind Finn, so

I missed the food parcel finally sinking into the loch's waters and disappearing for good beneath its glossy dark surface.

Before I could protest, Rosemary Tanner, another of the oldies, cleared her throat as though she were about to give a speech.

'Yes, better stand back from the water,' she said. 'You don't want the monsters to get you.'

'Here, here!' muttered Mr and Mrs Daniels, and Old Bill mumbled something too.

Mum pulled me back further still, until I was standing behind everyone else, enveloped in her arms.

There was a legend in Mivtown about monsters awakening from the loch. The adults used it to scare us away from the water, but we were hazy about what the monsters actually were or even what would raise them. All we knew was that the monsters were supposed to lead you into the water.

They were the reason why we were standing there on that cold, cold night, stamping our feet to stop the raw air numbing them, watching our breath unfurl like smoke from a chimney.

Every year, at the winter and summer solstice, we would throw a parcel of food into the loch. An offering to the monsters. Or 'a bloody waste', as Dad would say.

But me and Finn didn't really think they were real, and that winter solstice, as we'd gathered in the village hall, as was our way, I noticed that the only people who watched the parcels of cakes and tarts sink beneath the black waters of the loch were us kids and the oldies. Everyone else had stayed in the hall, and when we went back inside, their cheeks were flushed red like the glasses of wine in their hands.

Apart from Mum, of course. She'd come out when she saw that I was going.

Mum has never liked the legend. She huffs under her breath whenever someone brings it up, as though trying to get rid of something inside her. She doesn't really enjoy coming to these village things, but I insist on it. Otherwise we would be left out. The only family in the village not there.

I had tried to take Tommi, my little sister, out with us, but she refused. She was quite content playing by herself in a corner of the hall. Tommi's like that. She'll disappear, hidden in a little den, amusing herself for hours on end.

We weren't gone long that night, not really, but when we got home, Dad found that Buster's hutch was empty.

I didn't believe him at first and ran out to see for myself, checking every corner of the itchy hay for his furry little body, and after that I stayed out in the garden with a torch, calling for him and checking under bushes and along the narrow shadowy strip behind the garden shed. Even down the road all the way to Finn's house, which stood out, lit up and welcoming in the dark – until Mum called me to come in.

Because rabbits don't just disappear.

Do they?

Chapter Two

I couldn't sleep that night for thinking about Buster.

I kept imagining him, scared and alone, outside his hutch, which was dry and sheltered and packed with sweet-smelling hay. Sometimes I managed to doze, and in my half-dreams Buster would be with me, sitting contentedly on my lap. He seemed so real that I felt sure I could feel his fur between my fingers, the weight of him on my legs. Then, all of a sudden, I would jerk awake and realize that it wasn't real at all, that Buster was gone and I had no idea where he was. After that, I tried to keep myself awake.

The next morning, in the weak light of the winter sun, I searched the garden and lane again. Tommi came with me, both of us with stubs of carrot in our hands, calling and calling his name, until we got so cold that we had to go back inside to warm up.

Time seemed to pass in fits and starts that

day. The moments when I was alone seemed to draw on endlessly, but then, when Mum asked me to help her sort out the old Christmas ornaments, time suddenly sped up. At one point I saw the light dimming outside and realized with a jolt that Buster had been missing for almost twenty-four hours. How could it have been so long?

News about Buster's disappearance had spread quickly through Mivtown. Dad told Mr Lamb, who told Mrs Daniels, and after that everyone knew. There are only five families in Mivtown. There's my family and Finn's, and then just three others: Mr and Mrs MacGail, whose daughter Stephanie has grown up and now lives in Abiemore; the Lambs, who've just had a baby called Colan, who makes Tommi seem very big; and the Wells family, who have two little boys, Danny and Tom. And then there's the oldies, who run things in the village and make sure everyone knows everything: Rosemary Tanner, Mr and Mrs Daniels and Old Bill.

It was Old Bill who discovered the body that evening.

From the slow trudge of his steps on the path I knew it was Old Bill before he'd even knocked on the door. And there was someone else with him too. The brisk, light gait of Rosemary Tanner beside him.

Old Bill spoke to Dad in a low voice at the door so I couldn't hear properly, and then I saw him pass over a bundle wrapped up in a towel, not unlike the food parcel we'd thrown into the loch the day before. Dad turned to me, but his gaze was lowered, as though he couldn't meet my eye.

I knew then that it was Buster.

I felt paralysed; something like heat, or the sensation of being turned inside out, travelled through my neck and shoulders and arms and landed somewhere in my stomach.

I couldn't take my eyes off the bundle that Dad held carefully in his hands, and then I heard someone speaking to me.

'Effie? Effie?' the voice was saying insistently, as though someone were trying to wake me up. 'Bill found him by the loch,' Rosemary Tanner was saying.

I stared, unblinking, at her inquisitive face, which seemed far closer to me than it actually was. Her grey hair was knotted into a tight bun. I'd never seen her look any different.

Finn and I used to wonder if she slept with her hair in its rigid silver bun, and if she did, how she could possibly sleep. Not on her back because the bun would get in the way; not on her side because the hairpins would stick into her head. And what did that leave? Face down on the pillows? But how would she breathe?

It was one of the little mysteries of Mivtown that you tried to unpick because there was nothing else to talk about.

Rosemary Tanner tilted her head to one side, bird-like, as though she had seen something of interest. She muttered something under her breath that I didn't hear properly. Something about the offering. Then she flicked open the black book that she always carried around under her arm, as though she might start reading one of the passages aloud. Because Rosemary Tanner was one of the oldies, she had the job of writing about the village. She was called the village chronicler, but Finn and I liked to call her the Crunkler because we thought it sounded like a made-up monster from a story.

Finn and I had a half-dare with each other that we would try to steal a look in the black book to see what was really in it. Finn thought it might be full of cartoons that Rosemary drew of us all. It was a half-dare because neither of us thought we would actually do it. We were too afraid of what Rosemary Tanner might do if we did.

At that moment Mum came through from the kitchen. She flew across the room and shut the door on Rosemary Tanner and Old Bill so forcibly that I wondered for a moment if they'd been hurt.

She shouted. Something like, 'Enough!' or 'No more!' as the door closed in their faces.

'Tori!' Dad said.

'I'm sick of their interfering,' said Mum, reaching up as though to tuck a loose strand of hair behind her ear, although there was nothing out of place. 'It's none of their business, Kev.' She took the little bundle gently from Dad's hands and turned to me. 'Effie? Are you OK?'

I didn't answer her but looked at Dad and asked, 'Is it . . . ?'

'It's Buster, love,' he said. 'He's gone.' He came over to me and put a hand on my shoulder. It had begun to shake and wouldn't stop.

'Oh, Effie,' Mum said. 'Let me put him outside.'

Dad kept saying things like 'You're all right, Effie, you're all right,' and 'He was a good rabbit, wasn't he? He had a good life,' over and over until I stopped shaking

'It must have been foxes, Effie,' Mum told me. 'Poor old Buster.'

'Bustaaa!' repeated Tommi. She thought we were getting him out when she heard us talking about him. She loved him almost as much as I did.

'No, Tommi,' I said quietly. 'Buster's gone now.' It made it seem more real, saying it aloud.

Tommi looked at me solemnly, blinked a few times as though she were taking in the news and then toddled off into the living room.

'Can I go and see Finn?' I asked, and then, seeing Mum's face turn to disapproval, I added, 'Just quickly?'

Finn lived next door to us. I say 'next door', but Finn's house was a good ten-minute walk away. But it was the closest to ours and so he was technically our next-door neighbour.

That's what Mivtown's like. Our houses are scattered across the valley and around the loch like a handful of autumn leaves released into the wind.

Finn's my best friend in the whole world. We like to joke that we've been friends since before we were born. I even have a photograph of my mum and Finn's mum, Kathleen, standing opposite each another. They are holding hands, wearing matching flowery dresses, their heads turned towards the camera and smiling. The round, pregnant bumps of their bellies almost touching.

We were both born just a week after it was taken. On the very same day.

When we were younger, we used to wind each other up, saying that they'd mixed us up when we were born, that we'd been swapped around and no one had noticed. There's a picture of us when we were just days old and we look exactly alike – little wrapped-up sausages, side by side. Our tiny red faces are screwed up into identical grimaces, both of us shocked to be out in the world. We are wrapped up in yellow blankets so you can barely tell us apart, and this little detail only added fuel to our fantasy.

We would spend as much time together as we could, and whenever we weren't together I seemed to be locked in a battle of wills with my mum, asking if I could go and see him.

'Please, Mum, can I go to Finn's?' I asked again. 'Please. He'll want to know about Buster, and I—'

'All right,' she said. 'But quickly. Don't be too long, OK? You must be back for dinner in half an hour.'

I tore off down the road to Finn's and was breathless by the time I got there.

Finn opened the door. As soon as he saw my face, he knew.

'Buster,' he said. His forehead wrinkled with concern. 'What happened?'

'He was . . . by the loch. Foxes, Mum says.'

Finn's eyes filled with tears.

'Finn . . .' I said, but I couldn't finish my sentence.

I didn't need to speak. Finn just understood.

Chapter Three

Mum had given me Buster for my birthday the year before, when I'd turned nine.

It was a surprise.

'Close your eyes! Put out your hands!' she said, and I'd felt his warm velvet nose tickling my fingers; when I opened my eyes, Mum had placed him right on my lap.

'Happy birthday, Effie!' she cried, and I looked at the tiny fluffy brown-black bundle that was investigating my knees, and felt a warm kind of happiness that filled me up, right to the top. I had been talking about wanting a rabbit for a while but didn't think that Mum would let me have one.

'It's a big responsibility,' she always said. 'Rabbits need looking after.'

'I can do it,' I swore, every time.

'You must take good care of him,' she warned me again when she gave him to me. 'Make sure he always has food and water, and that you clean out his hutch regularly. And you must always, always shut it properly to stop him from getting out and the foxes from getting in.'

'I will, I will,' I said in a mantra, and stroked his ears gently back with one finger.

But then, on the night of the offering, Dad found the hutch empty.

'I'm sure I closed it,' I said, more to myself than to anyone else.

'Oh, Effie,' Mum said, looking anxious.

I thought that perhaps she didn't believe me, but I clearly remembered sliding the bolt back, throwing in the bits of carrot and cucumber, and then sliding it back across the hutch door again. I could picture myself doing it, as though watching myself in a film playing in my head: I had been in a hurry. Dinner was on the table inside. Steaming plates of shepherd's pie I'd run out on to feed Buster.

'It's dinner time, Effie,' Mum shouted as I ran through the door, but I was already gone, sprinting towards his hutch at such speed I felt like my feet were going to trip over themselves. I never liked to eat dinner if I hadn't fed him first.

'There you go, Buster,' I said, and watched him lope out from the dark bit of the hutch to start gnawing at a carrot. 'See ya, boy . . .' I traced my hand across the cage, testing to see if the door was properly closed before I ran back inside.

'I did close it, I'm sure I did.'

'Well . . .' said Mum, almost helplessly.

It didn't seem real: one moment he had been there, nibbling at that old bit of carrot, and then in another, he was gone. And he would never come back.

'We can get another rabbit, if you want,' Mum said when she saw my tears, but I shook my head. I didn't want to replace Buster. How could anything fill the hole he'd left behind? It only seemed right to acknowledge that gap, to test its edges to see how big it was, to feel how deep it went.

Dad came back in. I saw the mud on his hands; there was a smear that went right across his knuckles like a stripe.

'I'm sorry, Effie,' he said, and he opened his arms to me. I ran over and gratefully sank into him. He felt reassuringly solid, standing tall and straight as the trunk of the tree. Dad smelled of the outside, like the rain which had just fallen.

'Shall we bury him now? It's ready.'

'OK,' I said, and we walked out into our dusky garden, heading for the rectangular hole next to the hedge.

Droplets of water clung to bare branches, suspended and still. It was as though the whole garden was waiting for us to begin.

Dad lowered the bundle into the hole.

'Can I stroke him?'

'Yes, of course,' he said, but as I made to pull the rags away, he yelled out, 'Effie, stop!'

'What?' I said.

'Don't do that – you don't want to see.'

My hand wavered there for a moment or two, and then Dad reached forward and gently pulled my hand back.

'Come on. Help me with the soil,' and we covered him up with spade after spade of wet, dark earth until we couldn't see him any more.

Even as I was lifting another load of earth on top of Buster, I wanted to reach out and pull away the material so that I could see his dear old face just one last time.

But I didn't.

I stood by Dad, helping him fill in the hole until there was no more soil left and the rain started to fall quietly around us again.

'Let's get back in, Effie,' Dad said. 'Before we get drenched.'

'Dad?'

'Yes?'

'Was the hutch closed when you found Buster gone? Or was the door open? I was sure I shut it.'

'It . . . it was . . .' Dad rubbed at his beard as though he were deciding something. 'It was open, love. The bolt must have loosened or something.'

'It was my fault,' I said.

'Well . . .'

'I didn't do the latch up properly. It must have been me.'

'It's no one's fault, Effie. It was just an accident. That's all.'

I didn't answer.

'It's not your fault, love,' Dad said again. 'Come on, let's go in. Warm up.'

'In a minute, Dad.'

'All right, love. If you're sure.'

I stood out there for a while after Dad had gone in. The rain soaked through my coat and through my jumper and my shirt, but I didn't mind. In a funny sort of way I wanted to feel cold and wet because that's what it felt like in my head at that moment. Shivery, shaky and chilled.

I wished I had pulled back the old blanket to see Buster one last time. Without seeing him, it didn't feel like a proper goodbye; I hadn't been able to say sorry.

I knew Dad wanted to protect me, but what he

didn't realize was that because I hadn't seen Buster, my mind filled in the blanks. My brain threw up dark images that unnerved and frightened me, and I spent many sleepless nights wondering what had happened to Buster.

But losing him was only the beginning.

Can you imagine being kept in a cage? Seeing the world only through bars?

Sometimes I feel like I am trapped in one. It's invisible, but I know it's there. I want to break down its door. Run free. See the world double, triple before me.

But how can you escape from a cage that you cannot see? And what if that cage is the safest place to be?

Chapter Four

The next day Finn arrived at my house early, before I had even finished breakfast. It was the Christmas holidays and so we didn't have to go off to school.

I knew it was him as soon as I heard the precise *knock-knock, knock-knock* on the door.

'Finn!' I shouted, getting up so quickly that I knocked the kitchen table, and for a moment Mum and Dad's cups of tea and all our breakfast things quivered slightly.

'Careful, Effie,' Mum warned as I dashed to the door.

I flung it open, and despite everything that had happened the day before, I couldn't stop smiling when I saw him.

Finn and I are almost exactly the same height, so sometimes when we are standing opposite each other, as we were just then, it feels like I am looking in a mirror. We have the same colour eyes, a sort of hazel brown, and though my hair is much longer than Finn's, his flops over his forehead just like mine does.

'Wotcha Effie,' Finn said.

'Wotcha Finn,' I said back. That was how we always greeted each other. I can't even remember how it started now, but it always made us smile each time we said it.

'Fancy a walk?' Finn asked.

'Yeah, definitely. Give me a sec. Want to come in?'

Finn watched his breath smoke in the cold air and nodded.

Before Mum and Dad spoke, I said in a rush, 'Just going for a quick walk with Finn – won't be long,' and ran upstairs to get my boots and coat.

'Not so fast, Effie,' Mum said when I came back down. 'You need to finish your breakfast first.'

I grumbled a bit but sat down and chewed vigorously on the lukewarm piece of toast that was still left on my plate, while Finn showed Mum a cone that he had picked up on his way over.

'Where are the pair of you walking to?' Mum asked.

'Perhaps to the—' Finn started, but I interrupted him.

'Just round the village,' I said vaguely. I knew that was the only place Mum wouldn't object to.

'Stay clear of the loch path today, it might be slippery,' she added.

'I said we're only going round the village,' I said, more sharply than I meant to.

Mum didn't answer but took a swig from her mug even though it seemed to be empty.

'Can I go now?' I asked when I had swallowed my last mouthful of toast.

Mum pursed her lips together as though about to object, but then she nodded and I ran from the table, eager to escape into the cold, frosty lane with Finn.

'How are you doing?' he asked me once we'd left the house.

'I just can't believe I left the hutch open. I feel so stupid. I just hope that . . . that it was, you know, quick . . . that he wasn't in pain . . .' My voice died away.

We stomped companionably together up the path that led to the village. The nice thing about being with Finn was that I didn't need to speak for him to understand me – or the other way round. He knew instinctively that I couldn't talk about Buster, and I knew that he understood why I was feeling so wretched.

We looped through the village and quickly ran into Mr and Mrs Daniels, who were on their way to see the Lamb family with something to help with baby Colan's teething. Everyone knew everyone's business in Mivtown, whether they wanted to or not.

'It's one of our old Mivtown secret recipes,' Mrs Daniels said as she explained where they were going. She tapped the small, folded brown paper bag in her hand. 'It worked on the pair of you when you were teething bairns.'

We nodded, and when they asked us where we were going, mumbled something about stretching our legs.

'Shall we go to the loch?' I said, once they were out of earshot.

Finn looked at me slightly mischievously. He'd heard what Mum had said about the loch path as clearly as I had. Without saying a word, he took the fork that led towards it. He was as drawn to it as I was. It was our favourite part of Mivtown.

We rounded the corner past Rosemary Tanner's cottage, and the loch opened up before us. It was a sight that I would never tire of: it lay across the land, silver and silent, a mirror to the sky. The water looked so grey and still, it seemed as though it was solid and you could walk across it if you tried.

I had always had the feeling, perhaps because of the legend that I had grown up with, that there was something hidden within it, and that if we looked closely or long enough, it might give up its secrets. Maybe, just maybe, one of the monsters from the legend would rear its head.

As we always did, we stood there for a moment, unmoving. We watched the ripples travel across the water in their seamless, rhythmic way, and for the first time since I had discovered that Buster was gone, I felt a sense of calm sweep over me.

'See anything?' Finn asked.

'Nah,' I replied. The loch stretched out before us, unreachable and unknowable. 'I don't think we'll ever see anything from here, not by the edge. We need to get to the centre – we need a boat.' I was joking really, thinking aloud.

The only person in Mivtown who owned a boat was Mr Daniels, and it was locked up in the outhouse in his garden. Once, he and Mrs Tanner had offered to take us kids out in it, but our parents refused, thinking the waters were too deep, too dangerous.

But Finn turned to me, enthused. 'That's it! We could make one!'

'Make one?' I said doubtfully.

'Not a boat exactly, but a raft. I'm sure we could do it.' Finn's hazel eyes gleamed with excitement. 'What do you think?'

'OK,' I said. 'Let's try.'

He scrabbled around in his pockets and produced a piece of paper and a pencil, and started listing different ways to make the raft.

There was a moment there, as I watched him, my oldest and closest friend, hunched over the little piece of paper, his brow furrowed in concentration, scribbling away, when I completely forgot what had happened to my dear Buster.

Chapter Five

'Effie, Effie.' I could hear Mum's voice, but it sounded very far away – as though she, or I, were in a tunnel, a distance between us. 'It's time to get up. Come on now, love. Wake up. It's the Tindlemas.'

I blinked my eyes open; the glare of my bedside lamp hurt my pupils. Mum's face came into focus before me. She had pushed her hair behind her ears, so I could see her large brown eyes looking at me, a little concerned. It was black and still outside.

'We don't have to go,' Mum started to say, which made me sit up, dizzy but awake. I looked over at the alarm clock on my bedside table. It read 11:35 p.m. in glowing red numbers, and seeing that, I tried to rouse myself. There was not much time before we had to be there.

'I'm up,' I said. 'I'm coming.'

'Are you sure? You look half asleep.'

I yawned noisily and rubbed my eyes to make them open more fully. I'd never been allowed to go to a Tindlemas before; I didn't want to miss it.

It was the second night after the offering. At midnight at Tindlemas, all the villagers walk around the loch by candlelight. According to the legend, it's to check that the offering has kept the monsters at bay. Finn and I had never been allowed to go before because our parents thought we were too young – although at least one person from every family has to go; last year I had begged my dad for details about it.

'I don't see what the fuss is all about. Maybe we should all stay at home,' Mum had said, but Dad had raised his eyebrows at her and said, 'Remember the MacGails?'

Apparently, once they had gone away on holiday and missed both the night of the offering and Tindlemas, and the oldies were so angry with them that they stopped talking to them for a full year. Even though the other adults might not believe in the legend like the oldies did, they would rather go along with it than enrage them.

This year, Finn's parents, Kathleen and Rob, had said that Finn could go to Tindlemas, and so I had pestered Mum and Dad until at last they had relented – on the condition that Mum came with me and I held her hand the whole way round the loch. Dad was going to stay at home with Tommi.

I was hoping she would forget about the hand-holding thing once we got out there, but as soon as we left the house that night – bundled into so many jumpers and coats and scarves that I wondered if I would be able to walk at all – I felt Mum's tight clasp around my palm.

'Remember, Effie, stay close to me.'

The cold air stung my cheeks, making me feel properly awake, but I didn't reply; the only sound was the stomp of our footsteps down the road towards Finn's. As we got closer, I broke away from Mum's grip and ran to their door, hammering on it with my gloved fist.

I could hear Finn shouting, 'Effie's here,' and then there was a scramble and some laughter, and Rob and Finn threw open the door to us. I could see Kathleen behind them putting on a hat.

'Right, ready!' she said brightly.

I ran into the hall and hugged Finn, Rob and then Kathleen in turn, only noticing afterwards that Mum lurked awkwardly in the doorway as though unsure that she was welcome. But before I could dwell on it, Kathleen started ushering us out and Mum said, 'Let's go,' in a friendly sort of way, and we spilled out of Finn's house and started walking towards the loch. The stars were bright, clustered together in little groups, as we were.

'Effie,' Mum said warningly when I started walking ahead with Finn. 'Remember what we said.'

She held her hand out to me, and reluctantly I took it and fell into step with her.

We didn't talk much – maybe because it was so cold. It was the sort of cold that makes you forget what it was like to be warm. I could feel my steps become heavier as it seeped through the thick pair of socks I was wearing under my boots, numbing my feet and legs.

Rob led the way with the larger torch, which sent a strong white beam darting across the path before us; Finn had a smaller one that he angled backwards so Mum and I could see. It was still difficult to make out where you were going though, and in the darkness and the silence I wondered if we would ever get there.

Then I saw them – the glow of lanterns in the distance – and we hastened towards them. Even from afar, I could see the warm yellow glow of the flickering candles. The light was much dimmer than our torches and cast soft shadows around the group and the darkness that lay behind them. The loch.

I thought I felt the air get colder as we approached the loch. It was barely visible in the darkness, and I suddenly thought that we would not be able to tell where the bank ended and where the loch began; how easy it would be to fall into its waters, to sink beneath its surface.

Then I remembered that Rosemary Tanner knew the path that snaked along the loch edge – she walked around it three times a day – and told myself that I was just being silly, scared; that it was perfectly safe. But when I looked out into the darkness where I knew the water lay, I couldn't help but shiver.

The oldies were there, of course, handing out lanterns to everyone, and at least one person from each family had come. With a slight stab of annoyance I saw that the Wells boys were there, even though they were younger than Finn and me. Everyone was chatting, and I don't think they saw us coming because Rosemary Tanner gave a gasp of surprise when she saw us.

'Well, I never,' she said, and I remember thinking that I didn't really understand what she meant. She stood beside Mr Lamb, who looked like he didn't want to be there, lantern in one hand, the black book she always carried with her under her other arm.

'Hello, Kathleen, Rob,' said Old Bill, striding

over and bringing us a lantern to share. 'Young 'uns – Finn, Effie. And Tori – welcome.'

He held out the lantern to Mum, but she didn't make a move to take it – unwilling, I think, to release my hand. In the end, Rob stepped forward to take it.

'Hiya, Bill,' Kathleen said. 'Good night for it.'

'We haven't had a night this clear for a good few years,' Old Bill said.

'Seen any monsters?' Finn asked, and for just a moment I felt Mum grip my hand a little more tightly.

'No, nothing stirring tonight. But we'll do the walk anyhow.'

'Are you warm enough, Effie?' Mum asked me all of a sudden.

'Yes,' I replied, though I could no longer feel my toes.

'It was really freezing last year,' Rob said.

'That's right,' Old Bill agreed. 'We almost had to call it off because of the snow.'

'I remember,' Kathleen said. 'You think *this* is cold, kids!'

She laughed loudly, but not quite loudly enough to mask Rosemary Tanner's voice, hushed yet high-pitched, speaking to Mr and Mrs Wells.

'There's a first time for everything, but I didn't think I'd live to see the day *she* came to a Tindlemas.'

Rosemary Tanner's talking about Mum, I thought. I looked at Mum's face, but it was shadowy, unreadable. I couldn't tell if she had heard.

'Come on, Rosemary,' Old Bill said quickly, gruffly. 'Let's get this show on the road.'

Everyone started off around the black loch, but Mum didn't make a move.

'Come on, Mum,' I said, pulling gently at her hand. 'We'll be at the back. We'll be behind everyone else.'

She began to walk, but by then we were already trailing behind the group.

Chapter Six

Sometimes Mum and I fell out over the smallest things: maybe I was late home from the bus, or had left my plate on the table because I had gone out to meet Finn.

'Effie, how many times do I have to tell you?'

'Sorry-Mum,' I would mumble, the words slurring together as though they were one.

'You can't just run off like that . . .' Mum's voice would begin to rise. She would tuck her short fair hair back behind her ears, and then her large brown eyes would fill with tears. They would start to stream over her slightly pink, flushed cheeks, but she would make no move to wipe them away.

'Sorry-Mum, sorry-Mum.' I hated seeing her cry, but nothing I said could stop her tears. They trickled down her chin and fell onto her lap like raindrops, making a damp circle that looked like a stain.

I would look away so I didn't have to see her

tears; tears that I had caused. Tommi never upset her like I did – though I tried as hard as I could not to.

I remember very clearly the day Mum and Tommi weren't in when I got home and decided that I would go to Finn's, rather than sit in an empty house. I left a note for Mum, telling her where I was. I wrote it out carefully on a piece of paper ripped from my school notebook; I told her to call when she needed me home. I thought long and hard about the best place to put it, and ended up leaving it out on the kitchen table, held in place with a couple of mugs in case it flew away.

Mum never rang Finn's house. We started playing a board game where you had to go round a maze collecting things; it took a long time, and so I ended up having dinner with them – beef stew with buttery circles of carrots and a crispy-skinned jacket potato.

'Are you sure you can stay for dinner?' Kathleen asked me. 'Your mum's not expecting you home?'

'She'll ring when I need to be back.'

Finn and Rob walked me home later.

Dad came to open the door just before I reached it and I knew immediately that something was wrong. He stood very tall, filling the frame.

'Effie . . .' Dad looked grave. 'Your mum's very upset.'

'But I—' I started to protest.

'Just get in here and apologize to her, will you? She's been tearing her hair out.'

Mum was upstairs in the bathroom. I waited for her to come out onto the landing. I felt nervous, standing there, and I started rethinking what I had done that afternoon, trying to pick out the part where I had made a mistake. After a while, when Mum had still not emerged, I knocked on the bathroom door.

'Who is it?' Her voice sounded shaky and feeble through the door.

'It's me, Mum. I'm sorry,' I said, although I wasn't sure what I was sorry for.

I heard the lock being pulled back with a scrape, but the door remained stubbornly closed.

'Shall I come in?' I asked.

'If you want to,' said Mum, in a little voice.

I took a deep breath and pushed the door open. The light in the bathroom seemed too bright, too garish, lighting up Mum's tear-stained, red face.

'I left a note—' I began.

'Effie, you can't just gallivant off because you feel like it! I was worried sick when I got home and you weren't there.'

'I thought you'd see my note when you—'

'I did find it in the end, but first I almost tore the house down trying to find you.'

'I put . . .' I started to explain that I had put mugs on the corners on the note to stop it flying away, and that the kitchen table had seemed like a good place because she always sat there with a cup of tea – but I could see it was pointless. 'Why didn't you call Finn's? I would have come home straight away.'

'That's not the point,' Mum sniffed.

'I'm sorry. I thought you would just ring Finn's. I'm really sorry.'

'I'm not sure you are, Effie,' she said. 'I think those are just words to you.'

I didn't know what to say, didn't know where to look. I couldn't meet Mum's teary stare.

After what felt like a long time she spoke.

'Are you hungry?' she asked quietly. 'Have you eaten?'

'I had dinner at Finn's.'

'Oh right, of course you did,' she said, as though it were the ultimate betrayal. 'I think you had better go straight to bed then.'

I left the bathroom without saying anything and spent the rest of the evening lying awake in the darkness. I kept going over in my head how I had written the note to Mum so clearly, how I had taken extra care to make sure she would find it, how all my efforts had been wasted.

I was still awake when I heard my bedroom door open and Mum's footsteps coming towards me. I shut my eyes tightly.

Then I felt her hand upon my brow, stroking my fringe away from my face.

I rolled away towards the wall, my back to her, and grunted a little as though she had disturbed my sleep.

She left the room then, but not before I'd heard a sound escape from her.

The unmistakable sound of a sob.

Chapter Seven

'Your mum's having a hard time,' was how Dad put it when Mum and I fell out like this.

'I just keep making her sad,' I said.

'Effie, it's not you. Sometimes adults get sad about other things in their life and it makes them sad about everything.'

'What's making Mum sad?'

Dad frowned then and gazed into the distance – though he was just staring at the white expanse of a wall.

'It's not quite that simple,' he said in the end. 'But you mustn't blame yourself. Got it?'

I nodded, but one day not long after the Christmas holidays, when I came home from school, I could feel Mum's mood in the air as soon as I walked in – like a snake lying in the grass, ready to strike.

The air felt stretched and tense, as though it were harder to walk through.

'Here she is,' Mum declared to Tommi when she saw me. 'We were about to send out a search party, weren't we? How are you, love?' she asked, falsely jolly; and then, before I could answer, 'Where have you been till now? It's getting late.'

'Just . . . out,' I said vaguely. 'With Finn.'

The truth was, we had finally started work on a raft. We had sworn to each other to keep it a secret, knowing that our parents – and especially my mum – wouldn't think it was a good idea. We had just spent an hour gathering materials and talking about the different ways we could build it. I just wanted to see what we could find and take it from there, but Finn insisted on listing everything we needed: we made a start on it before the light began to fail and we were forced to go home.

'Effie,' Mum began slowly. 'You know how much I like Finn. You've got a good friend there. He's a bright boy . . .'

It was true that Mum and Finn got on well.

For one thing, they were interested in the same things. Mum drew flowers so that they looked exactly like they do when they grow in the wild for her job, and so she knew all about plants. She taught Finn about bladderwort, which grew by the loch and fascinated him. If we all went for a walk together, Finn and Mum would end up sitting by the loch edge, looking for the bladderwort.

'It's got these little traps – like cups with a door, filled with water,' she told him. 'Then an insect comes along, and if it touches one of the levers that operate the door, it will open, and the water and the insect are sucked into the plant for digesting. It happens just like *that*!' Mum slammed her hand down hard onto her thigh so that it made a smacking sound.

'Then, afterwards, what happens? To the trap? Can it be used again?' Finn asked.

'It resets itself. The door closes and it fills with water again. Pretty incredible, huh?'

'Yeah – I wish I could see it happen.'

'It happens far too quickly for a human eye to see – in about a hundredth of a second.'

'Can we go now?' I would ask pointedly, but then they would be distracted by a little fly that was about to land on the bladderwort.

There was one week when I was stuck in bed with a stomach bug: I was so weak I couldn't leave my bedroom, let alone the house, for a full six days. On the seventh day I came downstairs, my legs wobbly, my head still throbbing, to find that Mum and Finn had gone off walking together.

'Can I get you anything, love?' Dad asked me.

'No, I'm fine,' I said. 'I'll go back to bed.'

The truth was, I had an odd sort of feeling about it. When I looked out of my bedroom window, I could see Finn and Mum on the hill behind the house. They were passing something back and forth.

When they headed back down, talking animatedly, I saw what it was they had been holding: Mum's old pair of binoculars, which her father had given her. She had never let me touch them before because she said they weren't a toy.

I suddenly realized that the strange feeling I'd had was born of jealousy. I felt jealous of Mum for spending time with Finn when I wanted to; and also of Finn for sharing something that I never had with Mum.

I didn't speak to either of them about my feelings that day. I tried to bury them away, telling myself it was just silly – although at times their closeness still annoyed me.

Finn knew the names of all the plants that grew in Mivtown, thanks to Mum. When we were out walking, he would suddenly call out a name I didn't recognize and pounce upon some unsuspecting wild flower. He picked it very carefully, taking care not to damage it, and when he presented it to Mum, she'd beam at him, delighted, and together they would study the delicate petals.

'That's lovely bladderwort, Finn,' Mum would say, putting the yellow flowers in a little jam jar on our kitchen table.

She did try to teach me too, but I couldn't remember the names or see the differences between the flower heads like Finn could. Soon my incompetence turned to indifference. When I saw Mum and Finn talking together quietly, I tried to ignore the feeling that I was stupid, that I was being left out. Their heads both bowed in a certain way, as though they were a reflection of one another.

'Look, Effie,' Mum might say. 'There's some more bladderwort, like Finn found.'

I'd shrug, and the pretty little yellow flower seemed to shake its head jauntily at me.

So I knew that Mum liked Finn – but sometimes she seemed to get annoyed, cross even, when I had been out with him – or wanted to go out with him.

Whenever I asked if I could go and see Finn, it was as if Mum couldn't hear me. She'd turn her head away as though I wasn't really there.

'Mum? Mum?' I would say, louder and louder. 'Did you hear me? Can I go and see Finn?'

'I'll think about it,' she would say in the end, acknowledging me.

Later, I would ask again.

'You're really starting to annoy me now, Effie,' Mum would say crossly. 'I told you I would think about it.'

Sometimes, if Dad was in, I would ask him instead because he just said, 'Be back in time for dinner,' without even looking up from what he was doing. I would slip out through the back door, round to the road that led to Finn's house, and run all the way. Especially if Mum and I had had a falling out.

At those times I used to spend hours in their kitchen, as though waiting the argument out; waiting for it to wither into just a memory.

I would sit at Finn's kitchen table, and Kathleen would pull something warm out of the oven for us to tear apart. Currant buns. Banana bread. Golden, treacly flapjacks. Before I knew it, it would be dark and Rob and Finn would have to walk me home with a torch.

I never wanted to leave, though. Kathleen had to coax me out from under the table with her sweet, melodious voice; it sounded like she was singing, not speaking. She would pull me onto her lap and kiss my forehead.

'Come on, pet,' she'd say – words she usually reserved for Finn when he'd fallen over.

She'd tell me it was time to go but I could 'come again tomorrow, Effie, if you want to . . . And the day after that. And the day after that. OK, Effie? See you tomorrow.'

Rob would sometimes have to prise me out of Kathleen's arms with Finn looking on, his face creased with concern.

'That's my girl, Effie,' Rob would say.

'It's OK, Effie, I'd hear Finn's worried voice and bolstered by their gentle words, I would be able to leave them.

I felt at home there, you see, while the place they were walking me back to was somewhere else. Somewhere familiar, yes, but not home somehow. I couldn't help but wonder if they *had* got it wrong when we were born; if I actually belonged to Kathleen and Rob, and Mum and Dad were really Finn's parents.

But when Tommi arrived, beating her fists together and screaming as if triumphantly saying, 'I am here, I am here,' over and over, I forgot all about the silly stories Finn and I used to tell each other.

I had found something I was good at: I was good at loving Tommi.

I knew instinctively what to do to stop her crying, how to make her little round face crease into a smile, how to lull her to sleep. I didn't want to think that Mum and Dad weren't mine because if they weren't, then Tommi wouldn't be either. When I decided to stop thinking about Finn and me being mixed up at birth, I was relieved.

Because, I mean, you wouldn't want to grow up with a family that was not your own and not know it, would you? But there was another part of me that felt sad too. Sad that Kathleen and Rob weren't my parents.

And that made me feel guilty.

And quite, quite ashamed.

Chapter Eight

'I know how *close* you and Finn are,' Mum continued. 'But—'

'Don't go on, Mum. I know what you're going to say,' I said daringly, impatient for her to finish.

'What's that then?' she asked.

'You're going to say that we spend too much time together,' I said, the words tripping over each other, my cheeks flushing as I spoke.

'Well . . .' Mum said. 'It's just that it's dark now, Effie. You should have been home over an hour ago. Sometimes I think you spend as much time over there as you do here, and this is your home.'

'Well . . . well . . .' I blustered, and I could feel the words on the tip of my tongue. *Maybe I prefer it there.*

'I don't want to fight with you. It's just that I worry—' Mum started to say, but then she shook her head as though trying to shake a thought from it.

'Fine,' I blurted out angrily. 'I'll come home sooner. Will that make you happy?'

'Oh, Effie,' Mum said. 'Don't get so angry. It's just that—'

But it was too late. I was already angry. I could feel it growing within me like a fire that had just been fed a stack of papers. It blazed up inside me, fierce and tall and flaming.

I ran out of the room, up the stairs to my bedroom, and slammed the door behind me. Somehow that didn't seem enough of a barrier between us. I pushed my desk chair across so that its legs scraped and screeched on the floorboards, and propped it against the door.

I felt like I was trapped in there, as though I had been caged, so even when I heard Tommi babbling downstairs and ached to go down to her, I couldn't leave. I heard Dad come home from the distillery, and my parents' voices through the floorboards, but I couldn't make out what they were saying.

I sat on my bed and studied the most recent map I had made of Mivtown. I'd drawn in all the little places that Finn and I had discovered: the loch at its centre, and larger, at the bottom, our two houses, side by side. I traced my finger over the drawing of Finn's house, wishing myself there, rather than trapped in my little room. When I'd finished, I wrote my name on the edge of the map, in capitals: EFFIE WATERS.

After a while Mum knocked on my door. 'Effie, come down to eat. Let's talk.'

'I'm not hungry,' I called back, even though I was; my hunger was gnawing at my stomach insistently.

'Oh, Effie,' Mum said with a sigh. And then a small word, quietly, and so it was difficult to hear: 'Please.'

'I said, I'm not hungry.'

'You need to eat, Effie.'

'I don't need to eat! I don't need dinner,' I said, my voice rising into a yell. 'And I don't need you.'

As soon as the words left my mouth, I wished I could have caught them mid-air and stuffed them back in, but instead they lashed out with the force of a whip. All I could hear was a roaring silence.

I thought Mum was going to say something else then; insist that I open the door. I would say sorry, I didn't mean what I'd said, and go downstairs. I imagined sitting down at the table in front of a hot plate of food and feeling better. I even thought I heard Mum take a breath as if about to speak, but after that there was only the sound of her footsteps walking away, across the landing and down the stairs.

That was the last time we ever spoke.

Chapter Nine

The next morning I woke up stiff and hungry, to hear Tommi crying in her room.

I clattered out of bed so fast that I almost tripped over my boots that lay discarded on the floor.

'What's the matter, Tommi?' I asked soothingly, and cradled her to me.

Soon her cries turned to gulps and then to sniffs.

'You're all right, sweet girl,' I said, just like Mum did if Tommi or I were upset.

It was cold in the house and a chill hung in the rooms. Christmas had been and gone, and we were left in the cold part of the year when all the cheer has leaked away, waiting, waiting for the green shoots of spring to arrive.

I started humming an old carol and Tommi gurgled along with me and then she looked up at me and said, 'S'op now, 'Fie. S'op, S'op,' until I stopped singing.

'All right, all right,' I said.

'W's Mumma?' Tommi asked.

'Let's find her,' I said brightly, and took her small hand in mine.

'Mum?' I called out through the house, alongside Tommi's calls of 'Mumma! Mumma!'

I wanted to see her as well. I wanted to say sorry about the night before.

Mum and Dad's bed was neatly made and the old Arran jumper that Mum often wore was slung over the bedpost. The kitchen was tidy, just two mugs sitting the wrong way up on the draining board. But there was no sign of Mum.

'She's not here,' I said, more to myself than to Tommi. 'Must have gone into the village. Come on then. Let's have breakfast.'

I made us some toast and cut it into little triangles. I liked making Tommi's breakfast. When she was a baby and switched to drinking formula milk, I was pleased because it meant that I could feed her by myself. It was quite easy once you'd learned how.

Mum had let me do it now and again, but she watched everything I did, so even though I knew what to do, I got nervous.

'That's too much formula, Effie,' she would say, her voice rising a little higher with each word. Or, 'You've got to shake it really hard . . . harder . . . harder than that.'

I found myself making mistakes, and the more Mum tried to direct me, the more I seemed to do it wrong. Dad was the opposite: he always asked me to help when it was his turn, but he didn't bother looking as I made it, saying to me, 'You know what you're doing, don't you, love?'

I would nod confidently and enjoyed not having Mum watching over my every move.

When we'd finished the toast, Tommi looked worried, and craned her head over her shoulder this way and that, and asked me again, 'W's Mumma?'

'Don't worry, Tommi,' I said. 'She'll be back soon.'

But I was wrong.

Mum never came home.

Chapter Ten

The house was very quiet that night. Everyone had gone: the policemen from Abiemore, the oldies, the people from the village. Rob, Kathleen and Finn.

As soon as word of Mum's disappearance got out, the villagers had started arriving at our house. First Finn came with Kathleen and Rob, and after that, everyone followed.

'Just heard,' they said. Or 'Any news?' 'Terrible business,' they muttered under their breath.

Without fail, they had all brought something to eat – a lumpy-looking stew, a baked apple pie – and there were so many of us that Rob had to bring some more chairs from their house; even so, people had to sit on the arms of the sofa or cross-legged on the floor. It gave the whole thing the feel of a party or a celebration – it was wrong and misshapen, like the entire day.

It felt empty in the house now, without Finn,

not to mention the rest of the village, despite the fact that the three of us – Dad, Tommi and I – were still there.

Tommi took herself off behind the coal scuttle with one of her teddies, and only now and again did we catch snatches of her whispered conversation.

I heard her say, 'I love you,' and 'My vey speshul one,' and hearing her talk so tenderly to her battered old bear made me feel quite awful. Wretched. Raw in a way I had never felt before, as though every limb were exposed and aching.

I remembered the way I had spoken to Mum the night before. The terrible hardness in my voice, the sharpness of my words. It replayed in my mind, over and over.

Mum had been gone less than a day. I overheard the policeman saying to Dad that it hadn't been that long, but it didn't feel that way to me. Mum not being at home for this length of time felt alien to us all.

I could tell that Dad was worried in spite of what the policeman had said. A sort of mist had descended over his eyes the moment he realized that Mum was missing. It made him look different somehow, as though he were wearing a heavy cape that weighed his shoulders down. It made him talk and act slower than normal.

'Mum is coming back?' I kept saying to him when we first realized she was missing.

'Of course,' he said. 'Of course she's coming back.'

That evening, when I asked again, Dad stopped answering me.

Instead, I started saying, 'Mum is coming back,' with a confidence I did not feel, and Dad said nothing in reply.

Rosemary Tanner, who lived by herself in the small stone cottage nearest the loch, said she'd seen Mum walking towards the path that led to the water at seven o'clock that morning, and that was the last anyone had seen of her.

Because Rosemary Tanner was the last person to see Mum, she seemed at the centre of things; wherever she was in the house, there was a crowd around her. She looked small, fragile, amongst the others. For some reason Rosemary Tanner made me think of the small sparrow that Finn had found dead in his garden the year before, its delicate wings folded precisely, its body light in our hands.

'Why'd she walk to the loch?' I asked out loud when the house was full of people – the policemen talking to Dad in the living room, Mrs Daniels handing round a tray laden with steaming mugs of tea, the Wellses clustered near Rosemary Tanner like iron filings around a magnet, and Finn always, always beside me. The villagers had gradually appeared, and now they were all here. Congregating together as we had just days ago on the night of the offering. All but Mum.

No one answered me but Finn.

'Did she mention the loch at all? The day before?' he asked me. His brows were twisted, thinking hard.

'No,' I said quietly, remembering our last conversation.

Everyone spoke in hushed tones around me, but it didn't stop me from hearing what they were saying. Someone – I think it was Mrs Lamb – said something about Mum being unhappy, but when I spun round, she stopped abruptly. Mr Daniels, who rarely talks when we are all together, even muttered that Mum was 'troubled', but when I looked at him, his lips pursed together as if they had never been open and he looked intently out of the window, studying the panes of glass as though they were pages of a book in front of him.

After a little while some people began to talk more freely and Mr Wells said, 'I suppose it was inevitable. Tori was . . . well, she's always been a bit of an outsider.'

There was an uncomfortable silence. I looked over at Dad, who was still talking to the policemen. He was sitting oddly straight in the armchair and I wondered if he had heard.

It was Finn who moved first. He stood up, standing in front of me as though he could shield me from the mindless words, the meaningless chatter.

I stepped forward, next to him, feeling a strength I didn't know I had.

Mr Wells shrank back into the room as we stood there, looking at him, saying, 'Sorry, sorry,' his hands held up in submission, and in that brief moment, standing beside Finn, I felt as if things were all right again. It was the pair of us against the world. Together, I felt strong.

But then I remembered that Mum was missing, and my body was flooded with pain and confusion, intermingled in a knot that I couldn't untangle.

'It'll be all right, Effie,' Finn told me when we'd escaped upstairs. 'Your mum will come back.'

Every time I started to feel weak and sick about it, I remembered Finn's words. *Your mum will come back. Your mum will come back.*

I couldn't imagine that she wouldn't, and it was the only thing that kept me upright. It stopped me from falling over, as though it were a stick I had to lean on.

But Mum was never found.

They sent divers into the loch and they used Mr Daniels's boat to trawl it, but nothing, nobody, was found.

Chapter Eleven

I wanted to go down to the loch to watch the divers, but everyone had stopped me from going.

First Dad, who seemed to be talking to me as though through a fog. 'No, no, Effie, definitely not.' But he was still sitting on the chair he had sat on when he was talking to the police. It didn't feel like he really meant it.

I'd pulled on a hat defiantly, but Dad was staring at a spot on the carpet and hadn't noticed. I went towards the door, but Kathleen caught me.

'Effie, my darling, your dad said no – stay here with us.'

For a moment I stopped struggling and let myself relax heavily into Kathleen's arms. But as soon as she let me go, I made a dash for the door.

'Finn!' I heard her shout. 'Get Effie back!'

'I'm not stopping her,' he said. 'She wants to go.'

But Kathleen must have said something else

to him because before I knew it, Finn was racing along the path next to me.

'I can't stop you,' he said. 'I'll even go with you if you like. But I think you should stay with your dad. He needs you right now. You need to stick together.'

It was the first time Finn had said anything other than *Your mum will come back* and it halted me, hearing him speak like that.

'You think she's gone too,' I accused him.

'I think . . . something's happened,' he admitted. 'I don't know what, Effie, but something has happened to your mum. Something's wrong.'

I fell to my knees. The pain of hitting the cold, hard ground sent a shock through me.

'It can't be, it can't be,' I said. 'Finn, I don't want it, I don't want it, I don't want it.'

My words turned to meaningless sounds and then to sobs. I could feel them pouring out of my mouth. Something in me was telling me that if I cried hard enough, if I protested loudly enough, then I could make it not true. I could undo it just by willing it so.

I banged my hands on the freezing ground with all my strength, and then again, and again, as though the pain of my bruised hands could replace the pain in my heart, which was sharp and heavy and took my breath away.

When I had no energy left, I simply collapsed there on the earth. I didn't care what I looked like or how cold I was. I would have stayed there for ever.

Then I felt Finn next to me; he was on the ground too, an arm slung round my back.

He didn't make me get up or say any words to soothe me.

He joined me there, in my despair, and by his side I found that I could bring myself to leave it.

I can't stop thinking about that smallest of gaps, the distance between life and death. It means everything and nothing all at the same time. You could take a step in one direction, a moment too soon, a moment too late, and unknowingly you could be on the wrong path.

I don't see it in the faces of the others. They don't think like I do. They wear smiles because they're happy, not because they tell themselves to. They look at the world around them with wonder and amazement, as though it is a miracle existing for their pleasure.

But I . . . I feel terrified.

Chapter Twelve

I once heard a story about a woman living in the city who died in her flat; no one found her for three whole years. She was just sitting on her sofa with the television on all that time, but when the police finally went into the flat and found her, she had turned into a skeleton.

'How could nobody have found her for so long?' I asked, talking to myself more than anyone else.

'Cities,' Dad had muttered, in answer.

Cities. As if they were a plague.

I've seen pictures of cities, but I still can't believe they really exist. That many people, all packed together, brushing past each other's shoulders because there isn't any room left. It sounds plain crazy.

'I guess you'd never get lonely,' Finn said once when we were watching the telly: the grey, towering buildings and the jumble of people streaming down roads, as fast as the water swells the loch.

'I don't know,' I replied. No one looked that happy to me.

I couldn't imagine living in a place like that.

Here in Mivtown, there's not enough of us kids for a school. A bus comes to pick us up, along with a few other children from nearby, and takes us to a school of only about twenty kids in total.

When Mum disappeared, it sent a wave through the whole village. Every day we had visitors – sometimes the same people more than once. They all brought something with them – usually food, like a loaf of bread or a tub of casserole, but sometimes a bunch of flowers. Our kitchen table was crowded with bowls and Tupperware and all manner of things; there wasn't even room to eat dinner and we had to push our plates in between them all to make a space. It was as though everyone had to fill the gap that Mum had left. Most referred to it as 'that terrible business' with sad shakes of the head and a nod – or was it a bow of respect? – towards the loch.

One morning, not long after Mum had gone, I was at Finn's house when we heard something like a screech or a yell come from downstairs, followed by the sound of raised voices. We stopped what we were doing and leaned over the banisters of the landing to listen.

'I'm just saying, Rosemary, that sometimes people need some space, some privacy,' Rob said. His voice sounded strained as though he were trying to stop himself from shouting.

'Space?' we heard Rosemary Tanner mutter. 'This is the Mivtown way. If you don't like it, you shouldn't live here,' she said sharply. Finn and I quickly stood back as we saw the black-clad figure of Rosemary Tanner striding out of the front door and slamming it behind her.

'What was all that about?' Kathleen said, coming through from the kitchen.

'Rosemary and her rota for Kev and the girls. She wants us all dropping in on them round the clock.'

'Her heart's in the right place,' Kathleen said.

'I don't know. It's more like she just can't stand anyone disagreeing with her way of doing things.'

'There's that as well,' Kathleen said. 'You know what she was like with Tori.'

I knew that Mum and Rosemary Tanner had never been close, although I didn't know much more than that. I just knew that Mum didn't like Rosemary Tanner really. I noticed her voice would change in tone when she spoke to her at village things, but she never spoke about it to me.

But although they weren't close, after Mum

went missing, I noticed Rosemary Tanner standing alone at the edge of the loch, looking out over the water. Then, a few days later, she was standing there again. Not long after that I saw her again, in the exact same spot. It was as though she were in a trance or waiting for something to happen. It seemed to me she was looking for Mum too.

We were all feeling her absence. One day I saw Finn walking on the hill above our house; when I went to join him, I saw him looking about on the ground for something.

'Wotcha Finn!' I called to him. 'Dropped something?'

He shook his head, but his face was set, hard and straight. He looked upset, as if he were about to cry, but the wind was blowing and perhaps that was making his eyes water.

Later he confided in me that he had gone out searching for a flower that Mum had shown him once, but it wasn't the right time of the year, so there weren't any.

Quite often, Tommi would suddenly stop what she was doing and look around, asking 'W's Mumma?' just as she had on the first day Mum disappeared.

However, I'm not sure that anyone, even me, with my insides knotted themselves together at the very thought that Mum had gone, felt it more than Dad.

About a month after she went missing I came home to find the house empty.

I rushed from room to room, calling Tommi's name. Dad's. Tommi and Dad, over and over in an endless loop. But no one answered my calls.

I was quite alone.

I was about to go and look for them in the village. Part of me felt sure that they were there. They could have been taking a walk around the loch, as Rosemary Tanner did every day, or perhaps they had gathered round the fire in someone's house. But another part of me worried that they had left me too, like Mum had.

Just as I was about to head downstairs, I heard something in Dad's bedroom. It wasn't loud, more like a whisper or a sigh.

'Hello? Dad?' I tried again, and took a step towards the door.

I heard it again. A little shuffle. A tiny movement.

'Who's there?' I said sharply.

I was sure I'd heard something, but then there was only thick silence and I wondered if I'd been mistaken. Suddenly I sensed a movement on the wall, and when I turned I saw them, inching their way across: two shiny black slugs. They looked as though they were heading for my hand, which was resting lightly on the brass doorknob.

I shivered when I saw them, moving so silently, so stealthily, towards me, leaving a silvery trail that I could just make out in the dim light.

I was about to open the door, but then a voice called out to me from the other side.

'It's just me, Effie,' I heard Dad say thickly. 'Give me a minute, would you? Had a foul cold today . . .'

I let go of the doorknob as though I had been burned.

I heard Dad coughing and muttering to himself.

'You want a cup of tea?'

A few coughs later, Dad shouted a 'Yes' back. 'That's my girl,' he added, and I went down to the kitchen to put the kettle on the fierce blue flame of the stove.

I emptied the teapot and rinsed it out carefully, just as Mum used to, and when the kettle began to whistle, I poured the steaming water onto the tea bags so they floated up to the top, and fitted the tea cosy snugly over the pot.

When Dad came down, he looked a mess: he was wearing an old jumper that I had not seen in a long time. It was too big for him, swamping his body, and the cuffs were frayed and looked like they would unravel with a good tug. His eyes and nose were red.

'How are you, Effie? How are you doing?' he asked me. His face creased, wincing almost, in expectation of my answer.

I didn't want to tell him how I really was. That when I came home that day, I had feared to find not just Mum gone, but him and Tommi too. That I could no longer remember Mum's eyes exactly – though I imagined them full of tears because of something I'd done.

'I'm, you know, OK,' I answered. 'How are you feeling, Dad?' I put a hand on his forehead and poured him a mug of stewed tea, adding a small splash of milk, just the way he likes it. Mum was always better than me at making Dad's tea just right, but it looked the right sort of colour.

'I've felt better, Effie,' he said with a very small smile. 'Just need to, you know, rest. I feel so . . . tired.'

'Where's Tommi?'

'I asked Deidre to have her round today. She was very good about it. Said I'd send you over to get her once you were back.'

'Right,' I said, standing, eager to retrieve

Tommi from Mrs Daniels's over-tidy stone house. 'Why don't you go back to bed? I'll get dinner on for us. And collect Tommi. What do you fancy? Toasted cheese sandwich? Baked beans?'

'Sounds good,' Dad said. 'That'd be great.'

'All right then,' I said. 'I'll be right back. You go back to bed,' I repeated. 'Get some rest.'

'All right,' Dad said, but he was still sitting at the kitchen table when I went out into the dark to get Tommi.

By the time we got home, though, he had shuffled back upstairs. The mug of tea I'd made him was still sitting on the table. He'd barely had two sips.

I sat down in his chair and wrapped my hands around the cup. There was no warmth left in it, but I didn't let go. I kept my fingers wrapped around the chilly porcelain, until, sitting there, I began to feel very cold myself.

I couldn't stop thinking that I was the reason why Mum had left.

It was because of what I had said to her that last night. The way I'd said it.

I'd made her think that I didn't need her.

But I did. We all did.

Chapter Thirteen

After a couple of months there was a funeral. Of course, there was nothing to bury – Dad said that we needed to talk about it.

'I've got something to ask you, Effie. About the funeral,' he said as I sat down next to him. In the short time since Mum had gone, he seemed to have shrunk. His face had lost its open friendliness; his eyes were permanently red-rimmed.

'As you know, your mum's body wasn't found in the loch.' His voice sounded strained; strangled almost. He took a deep breath. 'The undertaker suggested that we choose some things to put into the coffin to bury. What do you think?'

I felt like I had swallowed a stone; it was lodged in my throat and I found it difficult to breathe.

'But what if she's not dead?' I said to Dad. It came out in a splutter. I couldn't believe it; I *wouldn't* believe it.

Immediately I regretted saying it. Dad's face

suddenly went grey and set, and he looked away. I felt like grabbing his face and kneading it like clay, sculpting it back to normal.

'All right,' I said quickly. 'I'll have a think.'

'That's my girl,' Dad said, and ruffled my hair before turning away again.

I felt numb as I looked through Mum's things. Her hairbrush and make-up bag were still by the bathroom basin, and I wondered if they had been moved since she had gone. I had been careful not to touch them, but now I reached out for them as though I might find a fragment of Mum that stuck to them. But they were just things, not like a person, and in the end I tidied them away into the bathroom cupboard.

I felt anxious about the funeral; anxious that I wouldn't be able to behave in the right way, even though Finn said that everyone felt like that and it was normal. It took me a long time to find things to go into the coffin. Dad had to ask me again and again, and in the end I only had an hour before he had to give everything to the undertakers.

I lingered over Mum's binoculars, which her dad had given her when she was a girl, but in the end I couldn't bear to put something that Mum loved so much into a box that would be buried in the ground. Instead, I chose the flowered dress that she'd worn when she was pregnant with me – the one in the photograph of her and Kathleen standing hand in hand – and also the bottle of perfume she used because its sweet, comforting smell reminded me of her more than anything else in the world.

'Are you sure, Effie?' said Dad when he saw the perfume and the folds of the delicate, flowery fabric.

'Yes,' I said, although I was reluctant to let go of the dress and the perfume bottle. 'She would want them with her,' I insisted, finally relinquishing them.

At the bottom of the box there was a large photograph from my parents' wedding: Mum's looking down so the confetti won't get in her eyes, but smiling widely, and Dad's squinting because he's already got confetti in his. I hadn't seen the photo before.

'Best day of my life,' Dad said when he saw me examining it.

'Where'd you get married, Dad?' I said, not recognizing the background as Mivtown, which I knew so well.

'Abiemore.'

'Why not Mivtown?' I asked.

Although there were only a few houses, we did

have a small weatherbeaten church that was usually locked but was sometimes used for christenings and things. A pastor came from Abiemore, and Rosemary Tanner kept the keys.

'We weren't living here then,' Dad said.

My eyes widened. I didn't know they had lived anywhere other than Mivtown. I thought they'd grown up here just like I had.

'Why?' I gasped.

'Well, we were both born in Abiemore. That was where we met. At school. After we got married, we lived with my parents for a spell, and then we wanted a place of our own, but Abiemore was too expensive. So we moved out to Mivtown. It was before you were born. You've only ever lived here.'

'What about the oldies?' I said. 'Did they move here too?'

Dad smiled – the first smile I'd seen since Mum disappeared.

'No, they've always been here. That's why they run everything. They are all related to one another.'

'No! Rosemary Tanner and Old Bill? And Mr and Mrs Daniels?'

'Yes,' Dad explained. 'Rosemary and Bill are cousins, and Deidre Daniels is Rosemary's sister.'

'So Old Bill is Mrs Daniels's cousin too?'

'Well, yes, I suppose he is.'

'And what about Mr Daniels?'

'Well, he's just married to Deidre, so he's not related by blood, just by marriage.'

'You know, it's weird to think of the blood that's running through their veins, linking them all together. Apart from Mr Daniels, of course. He's got different blood. Maybe that's why he's much quieter than the others.'

'Well, lots of them are connected by blood. You know that young Finn's related by blood to the Wells family?'

'Really?'

'Rob is Peter Wells's second cousin. And the MacGail family is related to the Lambs as well. I think they're first cousins . . . Lou and Alice. We're all linked up.'

'What about us, Dad? Are we related to anyone? Like Finn? Are we related by blood?'

'No, Effie. We're on our own.'

We sat in silence for a moment or two and I wondered how I'd thought for a moment that we could have been related to anyone else. Mum and Dad didn't have any brothers or sisters, and three of my grandparents had died before I was even born. I only ever met one: Granny, who had died when I was two, which meant I was too small to remember her – although I think I have a fuzzy picture of her in my head. Just a blurry pink face with a halo of grey hair around it.

'So, are you glad you moved to Mivtown, Dad?' I asked.

'Erm . . .' he said. 'Yes and no, I suppose.'

'Why yes?'

'Well, I'm glad you and Tommi can grow up with the green all around you. It's beautiful here. Unspoiled. And we all look after each other. And your mum – she liked the countryside too. And she could work from home so she didn't need to leave the village if she didn't want to.'

'And why no?'

'Well, I have to travel quite a long way to get to the distillery, and sometimes I worry we are a bit cut off here. What if I couldn't get home from work one day? That wouldn't be good. Sometimes I think we'd have been better off waiting until we could afford somewhere closer to the distillery. In Abiemore.'

'That's not too bad, though. You always manage to get home,' I said.

'Yes, I guess so, but maybe it was too much. Too isolated. Maybe for your mum . . .' Dad looked as though he were gazing through an imaginary window in the wall, which showed all of Mivtown. He wrung his hands together uncomfortably.

For a moment I thought I should tell him

what I had said to Mum. That maybe Mum's disappearance had nothing to do with Mivtown and everything to do with what I had said to her in our last moments together.

But then Tommi started crying.

'See to her, will you, Effie,' Dad said. 'I'd better get this lot to the undertaker before he closes.'

Dad picked up the box with its bits and pieces of Mum: the thin, cotton flower-printed dress, the glossy folded wedding photograph and the amber-coloured bottle of perfume.

Only after he left did I let myself cry

Later I wondered if I had used up all my tears that day because when it came to the morning of Mum's funeral, I found that I couldn't cry.

Not when, hand in hand with Tommi, I walked into the little church behind the coffin that Dad, Rob, Old Bill and Mr Daniels carried awkwardly upon their shoulders.

Not when Dad started crying when he stood up and talked about how much Mum loved Tommi and me.

Not when the first of the dirt scattered across the top of the coffin and Finn reached out and squeezed my hand.

I just couldn't cry at all.

Chapter Fourteen

Everyone thought that Mum had jumped into the loch that day . . . and had never climbed back out again.

Everyone but Finn.

'She wouldn't have left you,' he said. We were tucked away amidst the trees, not far from the loch, in a spot we had found one day when out exploring. The branches grew thickly all around a small, almost circular clearing; within it, you felt as if you were in a cave with green leaves, undergrowth and bushes for walls. We liked to think that the trees around us masked our voices. It was the perfect place for talking – and for raft-building.

You could only reach it by climbing round a particularly prickly gorse bush. There aren't many places in Mivtown where no one can find you, and I added it to the map I'd made of the village, calling it *Tree Cave* in small, cramped writing, with drawings of the spiky undergrowth and curved branches that grew around it.

'What if she thought I didn't need her? What if that really upset her?' I stopped hammering nails into the wooden raft that Finn and I were building. Finn was the only person I'd told about what I had said to Mum.

'People say things they don't mean all the time,' he said. 'She would have known you didn't really mean it. She knew that you loved her. And she loved you.'

I felt tears well up in my eyes, blurring Finn's face before me.

'She wouldn't have left you,' he said again.

We'd had the same conversation a few times now. When we first discovered that Mum was gone, I couldn't talk about it. I didn't want to say aloud that Mum might have left because of what I'd said to her. It was just too painful.

But Finn didn't think it was because of our last conversation, and that gave me courage: courage to find out the truth.

'There's only one way of knowing,' I acknowledged. 'We need to find out what happened to her.'

'We can do it,' Finn said simply. 'We can do it together.'

'If she didn't go into the loch, she must have left Mivtown, right? Otherwise we would have found her. People don't just vanish.'

But there were a few problems with that theory. She couldn't have left without a car. The only way out of Mivtown is by road. There are no buses, apart from the school bus, and it was a Saturday when she disappeared. Mum's old red Volvo, which was so rusty that you could see the road through a hole in the floor, was still sitting in the garage, untouched, next to Dad's car.

'Maybe she *walked* out of here,' I said to Finn.

'She'd have had to walk a long way,' he said, and stopped sanding the ragged bit of wood we were going to use as a paddle.

'How long do you think it would take you to walk to Abiemore?' I asked.

Finn scratched his head. 'About three days, I reckon; maybe two.'

'She could have done it. If she had some camping gear.'

'Rosemary Tanner said she wasn't carrying anything,' Finn said, scrunching up his nose as he did when he was thinking hard about something. 'But I suppose she might have hidden it somewhere. In the bushes or something . . . ?'

'Yes, exactly,' I said. 'She could have done that.'

'But it was January,' Finn pointed out before I could get too excited. He was always more logical than I was, grounding us both before I became too wrapped up in an idea.

There was no way that Mum would have camped. Our winters are cold and harsh. You wouldn't want to be caught outside even for a short time, let alone camp out on the hills all night.

'So I guess that means she's still here . . . But where?'

Finn looked over at me. 'I miss her,' he said simply.

I didn't respond. Finn had spoken the words that I couldn't bring myself to say.

'I just don't believe it,' I said firmly. 'I know we didn't always . . . but . . .'

'I know what we should do,' he said decisively. 'We'll retrace her steps that morning. Maybe the police missed something . . .'

I had my map of Mivtown in my pocket, and I unfolded it carefully on my lap. I pointed to my house and, using my finger, traced the path Mum might have taken. Because of the way the vegetation grew around there and how the paths were laid out, whichever way she went she would have passed one of the houses. My finger stopped on Rosemary Tanner's cottage.

'We should speak to Rosemary Tanner. She was the last person to see Mum.'

Finn nodded in agreement.

'Will you come with me?' I didn't want to see her by myself. She had a way of looking at you that made you feel odd, uncomfortable. As Finn had once put it, she was a little like a bird that has just spotted a worm. Inquisitive; hungry.

'Course.'

I got to my feet, dropping my hammer on the ground.

'Now?' Finn asked.

'It's only round the corner from here. Let's go.'

Soon we were standing outside Rosemary Tanner's cottage, knocking on the arched wooden door with its wonky lattice of frosted glass. I had never been inside, and I went up on tiptoe and arched my neck to peer through one of the little windows.

I could see a coat stand, and upon it the billowing black cape that Rosemary Tanner always wore; it reminded me of an eagle, hunched upon a perch before it takes flight.

'I don't think she's in there.'

'Maybe she's at the village hall,' Finn suggested.

He was right. We found her polishing one of the old, worn benches in the entrance hall.

'I wondered how long it would take you to come,' she said, without looking up, continuing to polish the wood, which looked almost black. Her hair was held back in its usual iron-grey bun, and her black book lay open on the pew beside her, a pen sitting on it as if she had just written something that had occurred to her.

Neither Finn nor I spoke.

'You want to ask me about your mother, don't you?' As she said the word 'mother', she looked right at me, and I felt myself go cold and sick at the thought of her being gone.

I took a step forward, though, and nodded. Suddenly Rosemary Tanner shut the black notebook with a thump and moved it away from us.

'There's not much to say, of course. Nothing that you don't already know. She walked past my cottage at about seven o'clock that morning, heading for the loch as if she couldn't get there fast enough.'

'Did you . . . speak to her?'

'No. It would have been quite impossible. I was inside the cottage; she was hurrying past. We didn't see each other on the path or anything like that.'

'And she definitely wasn't carrying anything?' Finn asked.

'Not that I could see,' Rosemary Tanner said.

'So she could have been? And you weren't able to see?' I quickly interjected.

'I don't think so. Nothing big, anyway. Maybe something small in her hand. Why?' Rosemary Tanner looked at us with narrowed eyes. In one quick movement, she dropped her cloth on the bench and stood up. 'You don't think she went into the loch, do you? You think she escaped. Left Mivtown. Packed her bags and left you.'

I felt myself go blank and weak. Mrs Tanner spoke as if what we were thinking was utterly absurd.

'You poor lamb,' she said, ever so softly, and came towards me. She held my gaze, and her eyes seemed fiercely bright, making me think of a hungry flame and the rigid stare of a hawk, all at once.

'You know, I lost my mother when I was just a girl too. But I still had my da, like you do. He was the most marvellous man – he taught me how to be . . . strong. That's what you have to do now, Effie; you have to learn how to be strong. You have to let her go.' Rosemary Tanner reached out a thin, papery hand. I thought she was about to touch my face, but she suddenly withdrew it, as though burned by something in the air.

'Well, thank you, Rosemary Tanner,' Finn said quickly. 'We've got to go.'

I was glad that he had spoken; I was immobile, voiceless. There was something about the way Rosemary Tanner stared at me that made me unable to look away.

'Come on, Effie,' Finn said, and tugged at my hand. We started towards the door, and Mrs Tanner went back to her polishing.

'There's just one more thing . . .' Her voice rang out to us. 'About your mother.'

'What is it?' I asked. My voice sounded small, not like my own.

'Your mother – she had the most terrible fear of our little legend. I know she wanted to hide it from you young ones . . . perhaps it's not my place to say. But she feared it. She feared it would come to pass.'

Chapter Fifteen

'Aaackygshgah,' Tommi screamed out. 'Squishy, 'Fie,' she said.

'Is it a slug?' I asked.

Tommi had already trod on two that morning. She'd lifted her little white foot and, sure enough, underneath was a squished black slug that had curled itself up into the shape of a C.

It was a small one – a 'bay-bee', Tommi had pronounced – but even though it was so little and so young, it didn't generate any sweet or loving feeling in me. Or in Tommi, and she loved baby things. Puppies, lambs, snails, seedlings, stones.

'Off y' go,' Tommi was saying to her slug. 'Off y' go.' But the slug remained stuck to her foot as if glued on, and in the end I had to scrape it off with a spoon. The biting air rushed into the house as I opened the back door; the slug writhed when it hit the hard, cold ground.

'Bad suggy,' Tommi shouted out into the

garden, wagging her finger and looking for a moment uncannily like Dad when he is trying to tell us off.

'You tell 'em, Tommi!' I said. 'Dad? I think we need to put down some pell—'

I stopped myself, seeing that Dad was not listening. He was looking at the cup of tea in front of him as though trying to decide whether to drink it or not.

'Dad? Dad?'

He looked up from his tea.

'I was saying I think we need to put down some pellets or something. To stop the slugs getting in.'

'Oh yeah, sure. I'll pick some up today.'

Dad and Tommi were going into Abiemore to buy me a birthday present. It wasn't that Dad had forgotten, but in the past it had always been Mum who organized stuff like presents. I had tried not to remember Mum giving me Buster the year before, and the way my bedroom floor had been scattered with presents when I woke up.

It was my first birthday without Mum. I'd told no one but Finn that I was sure Mum would come back that morning, the morning of my birthday. She would walk through the front door and sit down with us for breakfast, exclaiming, 'Happy birthday, Effie!' as though nothing had happened.

That morning my bedroom floor was empty. There was no card or bunch of flowers by my breakfast plate. I tried not to feel sorry for myself.

When Dad said that it made more sense to get me something I wanted, that I should choose something and then he and Tommi would go and get it, I made myself smile brightly. I asked for a globe or an atlas of the world, and while they were collecting it, I went over to Finn's for tea.

I kept myself busy that day. I didn't want to have time to stop and think about the legend that, despite everything, was growing in my mind. Every time we neared the loch I kept my eyes fixed upon the waters in case a monster was lurking there.

I couldn't stop thinking back to the night of the offering; I wondered whether we had done something different that had stopped it working this year. But most of all I thought of Mum.

I started to have the same dream, over and over: Mum was being lured into the water by the monsters, her feet moving stubbornly forward into the icy cold even though her mind was screaming at her to stop. She would walk on and on until, finally, her head would disappear under the surface and it was as though she had never been there. I would wake up then, sweaty and cold all at once, and tell myself that it wasn't real, that it was just another dream.

'So Tommi's OK?' Kathleen asked me as soon as I'd settled myself at their kitchen table.

'Ahm,' I answered through a mouthful of birthday cake. It was chocolate cake. Our favourite, me and Finn. Covered in dark, rich icing and decorated with silver balls that spelled out EFFIE and a lopsided 10.

'I did the ten,' Finn said, chocolate crumbs falling from his mouth.

Next to the chocolate cake stood an equally statuesque carrot cake with FINN written on it alongside another looping 10.

'She sleeping OK?'

'Mmm,' I grunted, although I knew that the dark shadows under my eyes told another story. With Mum gone, I'd been upgraded from part-time to full-time carer to Tommi.

Sometimes she slept so badly, I'd miss the school bus, and then Dad would mutter, 'Well, I'll tell Old Bill not to come in today then.'

Old Bill and Mrs Daniels were taking it in turns to help look after Tommi while Dad was at work and I was at school. We wouldn't have been able to manage without them, although I preferred it when Dad let me stay home or when it was the school holidays.

Sometimes I wished we could do it ourselves, just Dad and me. Sometimes I wondered if we could raise Tommi on our own.

I had my reasons.

For one thing, having them there made the house feel a bit less like our own.

I could always tell which oldie had been round that day because of the smell when I got home. If it was flowery and pungent, I knew it was from the perfume Mrs Daniels wore; if it smelled of bleach, I knew that she had been cleaning. But if it smelled earthy, smoky and of the outdoors, Old Bill had been there.

I didn't mind Old Bill looking after Tommi so much. He didn't move things around. Mrs Daniels was always rearranging things. Organizing drawers. She got into a habit of tackling one bit of the house each time she came round.

It started in the kitchen.

Anything chipped, worn or deemed useless was thrown out. Even if it was the cup I had painted when I was five. Or the funny little spatula that looks old and stained but is perfect for lopping off the top of a boiled egg. Every day I would find things missing, and when I asked about them, I always got the same answer: 'You don't want that old thing, Effie! I chucked it out!'

But I did *want them,* I thought. They were our old things, bits and pieces of our life when Mum was with us. If they were all gone, then what would we be left with? Would we start to forget her? I sometimes feared that I couldn't remember her face exactly.

'Tell her to stop messing with our stuff!' I cried to Dad one night.

'I can't, Effie. She's helping us out. It'd be rude.'

'It isn't. It isn't rude to say *Stop throwing away things that aren't yours!* Anyway, we don't need her help. I can look after Tommi.'

'Calm down, Effie. She's doing us a big favour. This place is getting like a tip.'

'No it's not,' I shouted. 'No it's not.'

I ran into the kitchen and slammed the door behind me.

The smell of freshly applied bleach burned my nostrils.

It was hard to admit to Dad that we actually needed the oldies' help; sometimes, even with Mrs Daniels and Old Bill helping us, things I hadn't noticed when Mum was there weren't getting done. Like our washing. Sometimes I ran out of clothes, and when I asked Dad where the clean stuff was, he looked at me vacantly, as though he wasn't sure what I was talking about. One night I had to put a candle in the bathroom so we could brush our teeth because we'd run out of light bulbs.

When things like this happened, I felt that I had to protect Dad, even though he was a grown-up and much bigger and stronger than me. I know it sounds silly, but it was like *I* was the one who needed to look after *him* now.

One day, when Rosemary Tanner turned up and offered to do 'a spot of cleaning or washing or whatever you need', I overheard Dad telling her that we didn't need any help. I felt a stab of annoyance because he had just run out of work shirts and asked me if I could put a wash on while he sorted Tommi out. He closed the door on Mrs Tanner without even asking her in.

'We're not that desperate, eh, Effie?' he said.

I smiled at him and shook my head. I was relieved that Rosemary Tanner wasn't coming round, but I was surprised that Dad had turned down the offer of help when we needed it so badly.

I didn't tell Kathleen any of this, though. She looked at me, lines of worry etching her face, and said, 'Have another slice of cake, pet. It is your birthday, after all.'

'I'd better get going,' I said. 'They'll be back from Abiemore soon.'

'Give me a sec and I'll wrap up the rest of the cake for you to take home,' said Kathleen.

Finn's mouth opened in a wide O. '*All* the chocolate cake?' he said, before he could stop himself.

'Yes, Finn,' Kathleen replied steelily. 'You still have your own.' She gestured towards the untouched carrot cake.

'But it's carr—'

'Finn!' she said sharply. Finn closed his mouth.

Kathleen turned to start wrapping up the cake.

I mouthed 'Sorry' to Finn, who mouthed 'Don't worry' back and shook his head at himself.

'Thanks for the flowers,' I said, and held up the posy of wild flowers that Finn had picked for me; it was studded with the bird feathers that he had been collecting too.

'Thanks for the notebook,' Finn said. I had given him a small one that he could carry in his pocket and use for lists and plans for the raft.

'Here you go, pet.' Kathleen handed me the

leftover cake, parcelled up in greaseproof paper and string. 'Happy birthday.'

'Happy birthday, Effie,' Finn said.

'And you too!'

As I closed the door behind me, I heard Kathleen's high laugh. 'Finlay James Paterson,' she was saying. 'Your face. All over a chocolate cake. What? You don't like my carrot cake, eh? You wee rascal!'

'I couldn't help it! I'm addicted to it!' Finn squealed. There was more laughter and then, 'Stop, Mum! Stop! Stop, please!' He was laughing. I peered through the window and saw them there, lit up, for just one single moment.

You know when you see an image, and for whatever reason you take a photograph of it in your mind? You don't know what happens next, you only have that frozen picture in your head.

The sun was setting and bathed them both in a bright orange glow. Kathleen, her mouth open in a wide red grin, standing with her arm raised as if she had just thrown something. Because she *had* just thrown something . . . it was the carrot cake! It was flying through the air.

Finn's face was screwed up tight, but smiling, the golden cake sailing towards him.

And the sound. Because with pictures you

take with your mind you can hear things as well –
they're not silent like a piece of paper or an image
on a computer screen.

The sound of laughter and shrieks and
screams.

I turned away from them and trudged back to
our house, which felt empty and cold – until
Tommi came bustling through the front door and
I buried my face in her downy brown hair. It
smelled salty and sweet. As soft as the tufty little
bird feathers that Finn had collected for me.

And wet.

Wet from my tears.

Chapter Sixteen

I couldn't stop thinking about the legend.

It was because of the loch.

Whenever we passed by, I found my eyes drawn to the ripples, every dip and shadow, searching for something as slippery and slight as a story. Or as solid and real as my own mum.

Finn would catch me staring and stand next to me, looking out over the water that moved and swayed and wouldn't give up its secrets. After a while he squeezed my hand, urging me on; if he hadn't, I was quite sure I would have stood there all day.

'You're thinking about it again.'

I had already told him how the legend filled my mind. I kept remembering the night of the offering, the Tindlemas, the make-believe monsters that we so carefully and religiously kept at bay.

'It's because they all think she went in there.

I wonder if anyone else thinks what happened to Mum had something to do with the legend.'

'Let's find out more about it. The legend,' Finn said in the end. 'We could ask someone.'

'One of the oldies,' I said.

'Rosemary Tanner would know more, but . . .'

'Old Bill,' I said firmly.

Finn nodded. We both liked Old Bill best out of all the oldies.

That day we walked home as quickly as we could – no lingering at the loch or popping in to inspect the raft. We came straight back, keeping our heads down in the pattering rain.

The first sound I heard when I opened the door was Old Bill whistling.

We went into the kitchen to see a rapt Tommi sitting cross-legged on the floor, watching Old Bill do the washing-up. He had soap bubbles on his head, wearing them like a teetering crown, and was, I'm quite sure, about to throw one of our plates in the air.

'Afternoon, Effie, Finn,' he said gruffly when he saw us. In one movement he removed the pile of soap bubbles and looked at the clock that hung on the kitchen wall. 'I'll just finish this lot and I'll be off.' He gave a quick smile, and dunked another plate in the hot, soapy water.

''Fie!' screamed Tommi in delight, as though she had noticed I was back earlier than I usually was.

'Hello, poppet,' I said, and kissed her on the head. Now that Old Bill had finished his performance, Tommi swiftly lost interest in the washing-up and toddled off into the living room, leaving just Finn, Old Bill and me in the kitchen.

I opened my mouth to speak, but then a funny thing happened: no sound came out. My mouth felt dry, my lips numb; I was nervous.

'Right, all done here. Cheerio, then,' said Old Bill, nodding at me.

Finn looked at me.

'Tommi been OK?' I asked.

'Good as gold, she has.'

'Great, great.'

'Well, I'll be off then.'

'Wait!' I almost shouted.

Old Bill turned, frowning slightly.

'Erm – can I . . . I mean, I wondered if you could . . . help us with something.'

'I'll try to. What's troubling you?'

'It's to do with . . . to do with . . .' But my words had got stuck. It was more difficult than I'd imagined.

Old Bill nodded but he waited for me to

elaborate, and I was struck by how rare it is for an adult to do that: to let you speak, without rushing to finish your sentence for you.

'The legend,' I managed to get out. 'The legend of Mivtown.'

Old Bill's whole face creased into a frown, reminding me of a list that Finn had finished with and had scrunched up into a ball.

'It's just that . . . I'm not sure, but I wondered if you . . . I suppose I just wanted to know more. More about the legend,' I finished lamely.

'Well, all I know, Effie, is what I was told as a boy by my ma and da. They handed it down to me, just as their folk handed it down to them, by telling us the story. Usually at bedtime, if I remember rightly. I've lost count of how many times I was told that if I didn't go to sleep, then the monsters would come for me.'

I nodded, remembering how Finn and I had teased each other.

'Your da's not a – how do I put it? – not a fan of the legend, shall I say?'

I shook my head slowly.

'Not many folk are, these days. But the way I see it, the legend was just a story to keep you young folk safe and out of the water. You know how it goes . . . the monsters will lead you in?'

Finn and I nodded simultaneously.

'Well, it's to stop children playing in the loch. To stop anyone . . . drowning. But the bit about the prophecy – I don't buy that.'

'What prophecy?' I said, my voice ringing out and sounding uncannily, I thought, like Rosemary Tanner's.

'The bit about what would awaken them. You've never heard that?'

Finn and I shook our heads.

'Well, like I say, I don't think there's anything in it.' Old Bill straightened a little uncomfortably. 'But the story goes that a girl born in Mivtown will awaken the monsters. A girl born after a boy. Twins. But we've never had twins born here since, and I hope we never do or there'll be no end to it.'

'Twins?' I said. I felt like I could hear my own heartbeat pulsing in my ears.

'Yes,' said Old Bill. 'The girl is supposed to be the one who awakens the monsters, and then they will lead us all into the water. It comes from a curse. A family in Mivtown, they lost their wee boy in the loch. He drowned. It was just an accident, a terrible accident. He was a twin, and his sister, she grieved for him terribly. She was there when it happened. She invoked the curse.'

'What are they meant to be exactly?' Finn asked. 'The monsters?'

'Well, I don't think there are actually monsters in the loch. But the wee girl, the sister, she thought she felt one in the water – its skin was slippery and cold to touch. But that could have been anything. She was traumatized by her brother's death. I think it was just her mind playing tricks on her.'

'So you don't believe it?' I heard myself asking.

'I think it's just a story to keep you young 'uns out of harm's way. I certainly steered clear of the loch when I was growing up. I didn't want the monsters to get me. But I suppose . . .' Old Bill paused. 'Well, as a wee lad I was told the story every night before I went to sleep. I mean, every night. I suppose I can't' – he seemed to struggle to find the right words – 'get it out of my head. But does that mean I believe it? I'm not sure.'

Finn and I looked at each other and Finn shook his head at me, so I didn't ask any more.

'I'll be off now then . . .' Old Bill said, clearly keen to escape my questions, before heading for the door.

'Effie? Finn?'

We turned to see that he had made it no further than the doorway.

'Yes?'

'Is there any particular reason why you wanted to know this?'

This was our chance to ask Old Bill about Mum. He might be able to help us.

'No reason,' I chimed. 'No reason.'

He frowned a little and then turned away, walking out into the rain that was still falling.

Chapter Seventeen

That night I took out the photograph of Finn and me as babies.

Wrapped in our yellow blankets, we looked identical. Could it be? I asked myself. Could Finn and I somehow be the twins? Was I the girl born after the boy; the girl who would awaken the monsters from the deep? Had Mum been led into the water? Was it because of me? Was she just the first?

Finn and I didn't have a chance to talk about it before Dad arrived home from work and it was time for dinner.

Dad overcooked the fish fingers: they were hard and dry and tasted more of the orange crumbs on the outside than the fish in the middle. I doused mine in tomato sauce, so all I could taste was the tang of the ketchup.

'Dad?' I said, in a questioning sort of way.

'Yes?' he said back, mimicking me.

'When Finn and I were born, who was first?'

'Finn,' Dad said, crunching up a mouthful of fish finger. 'By just a couple of hours. At one point it seemed like you were going to come at the same time. Rosemary wasn't sure what she was going to do.'

'What did Rosemary Tanner have to do with it?'

'She was the midwife – she delivered you both. Because your mum and Kathleen went into labour at the same time, and you both came quite quickly, there wasn't time to make it to Abiemore, and Rosemary was the only midwife here. So she said that they had to be in the same house. And when it seemed like you and Finn were going to arrive simultaneously, we wondered if we'd all end up in the same room!'

'Which house?' I asked, amazed not to have heard these details before.

'Kathleen and Rob's.'

'And we were born on the very same day?'

'I know – what were the odds? Just a couple of hours between you.'

'It is odd,' I said, thinking aloud.

Tommi started to climb down from her chair.

'Where're you going, Tommi?' I said, pulling her onto my lap.

'Down, 'Fie,' she said, and started to wriggle, but I wanted to keep her close.

'All right, sweet girl,' I said, letting her slide down to the floor. 'But don't go far.'

Tommi wandered into the living room and sat down by the doorway, just in sight.

'Do you think she spends too much time by herself?' Dad said.

I glanced at Tommi's back. She was talking to herself. Or perhaps she was talking to a collection of stones she'd found in the garden. Or to her favourite teddies, all sitting in a row. Or even just creatures she had cast out of the air itself.

'What do you mean? She's happy.'

'When you were her age, you never wanted to be by yourself. You and Finn were practically joined at the hip. You'd cry and cry until you saw him. Every day. It drove your mother mad.'

He almost put his hand to his mouth as the words tumbled out. He hadn't meant to say that about Mum. I tried to swallow my mouthful, but it felt like it had got stuck in my throat.

'I didn't mean that, Effie,' he said, before I could reply. 'It's not what I meant. It was just hard for your mum because . . . because you only stopped crying when you saw Finn. It was as if your wee heart was broken. But as soon as you saw Finn, you'd stop immediately. Like you'd flipped a switch. It was that quick. Your mother felt . . . well, she felt helpless, to be honest, Effie. She felt like she couldn't soothe you herself, you see. The only person who could stop you screaming your lungs out was Finn.'

'I don't remember—' I started to say, but Dad cut in.

'Of course you don't remember. You were only a bairn. I'm not saying it was your fault or anything. It was just the way you were. Whereas our little missus over there' – he gestured to Tommi – 'she just likes being by herself. We're all different, I suppose.'

Later, Tommi climbed up onto my lap. She was holding a tiny stone in each hand and she brought them together so they made a little clink.

Clink. Clink. They were so small, she really had to concentrate to make sure they hit each other squarely. Her forehead was furrowed with the effort.

Then she put one of the stones into my hand and closed my fingers around it. 'For you,' she said.

I suddenly understood how my mother must have felt when I was little. I imagined Tommi not beaming back up at me. What if, instead, she had looked away and cried, searching for someone else? What if she hadn't pressed a stone into my hand, but had thrown them across the room in fury? It would have been more than I could bear if Tommi had done that; if I didn't see her simple happiness reflected back at me. But I'd always known what to do to calm her, to settle her, to make her smile and laugh.

All at once I felt a heaviness that wouldn't leave me all evening. I slunk off to bed early, hoping it would disappear as I slept.

At some point in the early morning, when the darkness in the sky was still thick like treacle, I realized what the feeling was.

It was guilt.

Chapter Eighteen

The next evening I asked Dad if I could stay over at Finn's house.

'Just check with Kathleen and Rob,' he said. 'But that's fine. Sure,' he added unnecessarily.

I packed a few things up into a bag, along with the photograph of the newborn Finn and me. I wondered if Finn knew that Mrs Tanner had delivered us and that we'd been born in the same house; his house.

After all these years wondering about our births, were we about to find out that my most secret and greatest wish was true: that Finn and I had grown side by side even before our birth; that we were joined together by our very blood?

Of course, if this was the case, it meant that I was no longer related to Tommi. Or to Dad and Mum.

Unless my mum had been the birth mother

of both of us . . . but then Kathleen and Rob would not be related to us. That didn't seem right either.

'Do you think we are the twins?' I whispered to Finn that night as we lay in the darkness, me on the mattress on the floor beside his bed.

Earlier, as we were brushing our teeth, I had looked at our faces in the bathroom mirror.

'Do you think we look alike?'

Finn had spat out his toothpaste and then looked at our reflections. 'We've got the same sort of colour eyes,' he said finally.

'And hair too,' I said. 'Don't you think it looks a bit the same?'

'Perhaps.'

'I think so,' I said before Kathleen ushered us out of the bathroom.

'If we were twins, why would they keep it from us? And who do we belong to?' Finn asked now. 'Your family or mine?'

'I've always felt close to your mum,' I admitted. 'Really close.'

'But then, so have I to yours,' Finn said. 'She taught me everything I know about plants and birds and everything. It could have been the other way round.'

'But you look just like your mum and dad,' I

said. 'You have to be theirs. I don't look much like anyone.'

'I don't know,' Finn said. 'I used to think you looked like your mum.'

'Really?'

'Not a lot, but there's something about your eyes.'

'Well, do you think we should ask your mum? I don't reckon my dad knows anything about it. He just thinks we were born on the same day, a few hours apart.'

'Or Rosemary Tanner,' mused Finn. 'We could ask her. She must know. But if we were twins, why would they separate us? Why wouldn't they let us both stay with our real family?'

'Something bad must have happened, don't you think? We know that both our mums were pregnant. There's that photograph of them. What if . . . What if one of them lost their baby and the other one had twins, so . . .'

'They gave one of the twins away?' Finn finished for me, sounding dubious. 'I don't know.'

I heard him roll over onto his side; when he spoke next, I knew he was facing me.

'It would mean that you are going to awaken the monsters, Effie. If it were true; if the prophecy is true.'

'Lots of ifs . . . Finn, do you think it has anything to do with my mum? The way she went . . . like she did?'

I heard him take a deep breath in the darkness, but suddenly the bedroom door was flung open and we were bathed in the golden light from the landing.

'Sleep, you two,' Kathleen hushed. 'Don't be up all night talking. You've got school tomorrow.'

We fell silent.

'Goodnight,' she said, and shut the door behind her.

I heard Finn shift, turning over onto his back.

'I think it might,' I whispered to him.

But he didn't answer.

I didn't know if it was because he hadn't heard me or because he was too scared to say.

There is something within me. A stirring. I think of a whirlwind whipping up everything in its path; things come to land in a completely different place to where they started, the wrong way up from where they were.

Maybe I can change things too.

Maybe I can turn things upside down.

Chapter Nineteen

A couple of days after that, Finn and I set ourselves up in the Tree Cave for a full day of raft-building. I had risen early and given Tommi her breakfast, but although I was eager to leave, Dad was not yet up.

In the end I knocked on his bedroom door and tiptoed in. He was lying very still, and I noticed that his duvet was the wrong way round: the side with the buttons was at the top.

'Dad? Are you awake? Dad?'

He didn't answer.

I pulled the curtains back a little, letting the weak, thin winter light into the room.

'Dad? Can you look after Tommi? Can I go and see Finn? Dad?'

I thought he was still asleep, but suddenly his voice filled the room.

'Just give me a moment, Effie,' he said. He sounded tired.

I started to backtrack: 'Only if it's OK. Don't worry if it's not.'

Dad sat up and yawned noisily. I looked at him carefully: he looked thinner. His face was sharper – it had lost its roundness and I realized I had not seen him smile for a long time.

''S OK. Just need to get up. It's fine.'

'Are you sure?' I felt guilty leaving him when he looked so thin and unhappy.

'I'm up now, Effie. You're free.'

I went down to the kitchen and opened one of the cupboards. The last few Jammie Dodgers had gone soft but I took them anyway, and I made some sandwiches using up the very last of the peanut butter and Marmite, leaving one on a plate for Dad. When I got to the Tree Cave, I was glad to see Finn's offering of two thick cheese and chutney sandwiches and a tin of sticky, falling-apart flapjacks. The idea was that we would not have to go home for lunch – although we somehow managed to eat most of the food before the morning was out. Finn said it was OK because we needed the energy.

We had already built a square frame and were fixing planks across it to make a floor. Finn had made it look easy, but I was struggling. I kept missing the nail or hammering it in crooked. More often than not, I had to wrench my nail out and start again with a new one.

Still, I liked the sound of the hammer. It stopped me from having to think about things. Mum. The funeral. The legend. Dad, sad and lonely.

Finn looked like he didn't want to think about things either; as soon as he had secured one plank, he reached out for another and starting hammering. I wondered if he was trying not to think the very same thing as me: that we hadn't been able to find out what happened to Mum.

I brought my hammer down with a resounding, heavy thud. The nail bent awkwardly; I sighed and started to pull it out with the claw of my hammer when I noticed the absence of banging. Finn had stopped too. The quiet of the day settled around us.

'I think I heard something,' Finn said. 'A car door. It might be Rosemary Tanner.'

We had purposefully left hammering the planks for a day when Rosemary Tanner was out. Her house was nearest and we didn't want to give away the location of the Tree Cave by making too much noise.

'Let's have a look,' I said, and we put down

our hammers and crept through the undergrowth, round to the path that led to her cottage.

As we were about to emerge from the scrub, Finn put his hand out to stop me – and before I could object, I saw Rosemary Tanner striding straight past us. She hadn't seen us, but if we had come out only moments before, then we would have walked straight into her.

'She's off on her walk,' I whispered to Finn.

'No she's not. Look – she's stopped.'

Sure enough, she had come to a standstill at the edge of the loch.

'What's she looking for?' I said to Finn. She was gazing out over the water, just as she had in the days after Mum had gone missing – but there was nothing to see. Just water.

We peered out at Rosemary Tanner. She looked as she always did: the black cape; the black notebook clutched to her chest.

Suddenly she bent down, as if noticing something in the water, but there was nothing there, and after a moment she straightened up again.

'Come on,' Finn said after a while, in a whisper. 'Let's go.'

We scrambled back through the bushes until

we were encircled by the leaves and branches of the Tree Cave.

'It seemed like . . . she was looking for something—' I started to say – but then a thought planted itself in my head. A thought that scared me; a thought that sprouted, grew.

'I know it might sound silly, but maybe it's the . . . something to do with—' Finn started.

But I finished the sentence for him.

'The legend.'

Chapter Twenty

''Nother 'gie!' came Tommi's cry.

'Not another one!' I was getting fed up with catapulting them into the garden. 'Dad! There's another slug!'

'Put it outside!' came Dad's reply.

I'd lost count of how many I had evicted. Dad had put salt down, but it hadn't stopped them coming in.

The slug curled into itself as I tried to scrape it onto a spoon.

'Got you!' I said triumphantly, and shook it off into the grass, but as soon as I went back in, I caught a movement in the corner of my eye. Another four slugs, all different sizes, that I had missed. They were climbing all over Mum's old binoculars.

I picked up the binoculars by the leather strap, reluctant to touch their slimy, shiny bodies. Their skin glistened black.

One by one I spooned off each slug and ejected them out of the window. 'Dad?' I called out. 'What're Mum's binoculars doing down here? Did you get them out?'

The last time I'd seen them was when Dad asked me to choose things for Mum's coffin; I'd left them on her desk in their bedroom, next to a book about wild birds.

'I brought them down,' Dad said, appearing at the kitchen door. He had his coat on, but wasn't wearing any shoes. 'I thought Finn might want to have them. What do you think?'

'What do you mean?'

'Well, I thought we should start putting some bits and pieces of your mum's away – I remembered young Finn liking these. What do you think? You never use them, do you?'

'No, no,' I spluttered. 'And Finn will use them all the time. Birds and stuff. That was their thing.'

Memories of Mum and Finn filled my head: the last time I remembered them being together on one of their nature walks. They were bent, almost conspiratorially, over a leaf skeleton that Finn had found.

'These act like our veins, bringing water and food to the leaf,' Mum said, pointing out the tiny lines.

'Tori! I see a hawk,' Finn said, and quickly passed her the binoculars that hung around his neck; Mum had to bend slightly awkwardly to look through them.

'Good spot, Finn!' she said admiringly, gazing at the hawk circling the expanse of blue above.

'All right, love,' Dad said. 'Well, would you like to give them to him? I've got to be off.' He quickly ducked down and planted a kiss on Tommi's head and then one on mine, and rushed towards the front door. 'It's Deidre today, I think,' he added.

'No, it's Old Bill,' I corrected him.

'Oh yes . . . Losing track of the days.'

'Dad?'

'Yes, love?'

'Your shoes!'

'Ah. Oh yes, of course.'

Dad quickly shoved on his boots and left the house with a slam of the door that made the windows rattle.

Not long after, I heard Old Bill trudging up to the path. Tommi must have heard him too, for she ran towards the door, calling, 'Bill, Bill!'

I felt nervous about seeing Old Bill again after speaking about the legend, but I let the door swing wide and Tommi almost ran straight into him. He quickly knelt down and lifted her high in the air. Tommi's laughter spilled out.

'Flying today then, young Tommi?' Old Bill said when he put her down. 'We'll do plenty of flying today.'

'I'll be off,' I said, slinging Mum's binoculars over my shoulder, where they banged painfully against my hip bone. 'Bye, Tom.'

'Bye-bye, 'Fie,' said Tommi. Old Bill lifted her up so that she could wave to me over the hedgerow, until I rounded the corner and could see her no longer.

I caught up with Finn by the old crab apple tree beside the road.

'She wanted you to have them,' I replied when he shook his head at Mum's binoculars and said, 'No, Effie. They're yours. Or Tommi's when she's grown. I couldn't.'

'Honestly, Finn,' I said, trying to hand them to him as we walked towards the bus stop. 'It's right for you to have them. I know you'll use them properly. No point in them just gathering dust at our house.'

Finn hesitated, and I knew then that he would take them.

'You and Mum did a lot of bird watching, didn't you? She'd want you to keep going. Please, Finn.'

He took them carefully from me and hooked

them over his head. 'But if you ever want them back, any time, you just say. I'll just look after them for you until then.'

Finn started to peer through the binoculars into the sky, carefully adjusting the lenses.

'See anything?'

'Look – there's a buzzard!'

'You're joking!'

'I'm not. Here, have a look!' Finn quickly passed the binoculars to me. 'Over there!'

'Nope . . . just sky,' I said. 'Nothing there.'

'Next time,' Finn said meaningfully.

'One thing I should tell you about those binoculars, though.'

'What's that?'

'This morning they were covered in slugs!'

'What?'

'There were four of them sliming all over it.'

'I wonder what they were doing there.' Finn turned the binoculars over in his hands, studying them closely.

'What do you mean?'

'Well, slugs live in damp places and like to eat rotting things. None of which they would find on a pair of binoculars. It's just odd, that's all. You said they just started coming into the house all of a sudden?'

'Yeah – just the other day, out of nowhere. Our house isn't damp, and Mrs Daniels won't let anything rotting survive there.'

'See if you can find out where they're getting in,' Finn suggested. 'There must be a hole or something.'

The school bus pulled up, steaming, at the side of the road, and we forgot all about the slugs and the binoculars until the very next day, when something even odder happened.

Chapter Twenty-one

'There, on my bookcase. By the bird books. Do you see?'

Two giant black slugs were creeping over the lenses of Mum's old binoculars.

'Just like yesterday,' I said.

'How weird is that?' Finn said.

'They were black ones yesterday too.'

'Now, what's even more strange – this morning, when I woke up, I saw the slugs there and took them outside,' Finn told me. 'Dad said I had to put them a really long way away so they wouldn't come back in. I walked all the way to the other side of the village.'

I nodded.

'Then I put the binoculars back on the shelf, gave them a wipe to get the slime off and had breakfast. When I came back, guess what I found?'

'More slugs,' I said, my stomach turning over

as the slimy bodies of the slugs slowly wrapped themselves around Mum's binoculars.

'Exactly. But different ones. These were a bit smaller than the ones in the morning. So I got rid of them . . . And now it's happened again.'

'They like the binoculars,' I concluded.

'Yes, exactly. They're drawn to them. That's why they're coming in.'

'But why?'

Finn puckered his nose in thought. 'I don't know. But there's one way of finding out for sure.'

'Finding out what?'

'If it's the binoculars or not.' Finn's steady brown eyes fixed on the idea as though he could see it before him. 'We just have to keep putting them in different places and see whether the slugs find them . . . not just in your house or my house but all over Mivtown. We could start with the Tree Cave. We'll leave them there overnight and see what happens.'

Finn went to pick up the binoculars, but hesitated when he saw that they were coated in slime.

I opened Finn's window, picked up the binoculars by the strap and, using the metal ruler from the desk, flicked the slugs out of the window, one after the other.

'You get used to them,' I said grimly.

'Well, if it's the binoculars, then we keep them away from us and we won't have to!' Finn said triumphantly.

But later that afternoon I disproved Finn's theory of the slugs only being drawn to Mum's binoculars.

Tommi suddenly shouted out to me, 'Suggies! Suggies, Effie!'

I looked up from my homework and saw them straight away.

Slugs. One fat black one was trailing across the kitchen wall; three smaller ones were working their way round the skirting board.

It wasn't just Mum's binoculars; something else was attracting them. I looked around to see if they were heading towards anything in particular. They were in the corner of the room where I was doing my homework.

'Slugs,' I said to Tommi. 'They're slugs.'

'Suggies,' Tommi parroted back.

'Close enough,' I said.

I picked up a dirty spoon from the sink, scraped the fat one off the wall and slung it out into the garden. I should probably have dumped it a long way down the lane. Finn had told me that slugs have an incredibly strong homing instinct: if

I just chucked them in the garden they would definitely find their way back in, but I was looking after Tommi until Dad got back from work.

I scooped up the other three slugs so they were piled on top of each other in a writhing black pile.

'And stay out,' I said, my breath making smoke in the cold air. I catapulted them out but let go of the spoon too; it clattered onto the stone path. I looked at Tommi. She was sitting on the big armchair with her teddies in a row, talking to them very seriously.

I stepped out into the garden and retrieved the spoon, shaking off the slugs. They disappeared into the long grass.

It was that time of the day just after sunset but before it's dark. In those few moments it's like the world is wearing a veil.

I was standing near where we'd buried poor old Buster. The ground had settled into a patch of mud now. No one would guess what was there.

I glanced back through the window. Tommi was still talking to her teddies; she was wagging her finger at them, as if telling them off.

I turned back to Buster's grave.

Suddenly I thought I saw something . . . Something shifting slightly under the earth – just a flicker of movement, like the second hand of a clock, except without rhythm and order.

I walked over to the garden shed and lugged out the heavy spade, dragging it across the grass towards the hedge.

I couldn't help thinking that it was Buster under there, wanting to escape. That he had been waiting for me all this time, that I hadn't lost him after all.

I started to dig.

Chapter Twenty-two

Soon I had a large pile of earth mounting up next to me, and I'd cleared away the top layer of the hole in which Buster lay. The ground opened up in front of me like a scar, clods of soil, tufts of grass and white clusters of root.

It was only a pile of earth and a hole in the ground, just like the ones that Finn and I used to dig at the end of the garden. Nothing more, nothing less. Perhaps I'd imagined something moving; perhaps it was a large insect or a trick of the light. It wasn't Buster – I could see that now.

I stopped digging and looked at the hole in front of me. It felt like only moments had passed since I stood here next to Dad when we buried Buster.

And then, at that very moment, I saw something else move.

In Buster's grave.

In the soil.

Something dark and shadowy; I couldn't see where it began and where it ended.

Every part of me turned cold. I understood for the first time what people meant when they said, 'I froze.' It's not just about standing really still. It's because the very inside of you, from the top of your head to the soles of your feet, is instantly chilled.

I started backing away, although I knew I couldn't leave without seeing what it was. I didn't want to be haunted by dark imaginings of what it could have been. I needed to see for myself.

The light had faded now. Darkness had crept around me. I made my way back to the shed. I had to feel around for the torch that we kept on the back of the door, hurting my hand on the sharp nail it was hanging on.

I began to panic as I grappled for the on button – until the torch's thin beam illuminated the dark garden. But it was a feeble light: the batteries were dying.

I could hear Tommi singing now. She hadn't even noticed that I wasn't there.

My feet had rooted themselves to the ground. 'Keep walking,' I told myself.

I crept back towards the grave, shining the pale yellow light in front of me.

A metre away, I saw it again.

Moving.

Writhing.

In the soil.

The light was growing faint.

I leaned forward, pointing the dying light towards the earth.

The torch flickered. And went out.

Chapter Twenty-three

I think I might have stopped breathing. You know when you hold your breath and your chest begins to hurt? I think that's what happened. Only for a few dark moments, though, because suddenly the garden was illuminated by yellow light that streamed out of the kitchen window. And I saw for myself what was moving in the darkness of Buster's grave.

The hole I'd dug was full of writhing black slugs.

Chapter Twenty-four

I screamed. So loudly that Dad ran out of the kitchen.

'Effie! Effie! What are you doing out here?'

I closed my eyes and let my head sink onto Dad's chest. His shirt smelled musty. It comforted me, but even when I shut my eyes, I could still see the slugs. Twisting and twisted, in one moving black mass.

'Slugs,' I said into his shirt so he couldn't hear what I was saying.

'What's that, love?'

'There's slugs, Dad. In Buster's grave.'

Dad looked over to where we had buried Buster and frowned – two lines, so deep that they looked like they would always remain on his forehead.

'Get inside, Effie,' he said.

'But—' I started to say.

'Please, Effie, get inside. I don't know why you're doing this.'

I limped towards the warm light of the kitchen, feeling defeated not only by what I had seen in Buster's grave but by Dad's words. My body felt hunched and raw, as if I had fallen over and hurt myself, and I couldn't stop crying.

'Andda yooo, andda yoo, andda yoo,' chirruped Tommi. She was still talking to her toys.

I sat down on the floor beside her. I could hear Dad shovelling the soil back into the hole I'd dug. It made a sort of whooshing sound as he scooped up a shovelful, and then a *pitter, pitter, pitter* as the soil was sprinkled into the hole.

Whoosh. Pitter, pitter, pitter.

Whoosh. Pitter, pitter, pitter.

Whoosh. Pitter, pitter, pitter.

All of a sudden, out of the corner of my eye, I saw a movement. Something was there that hadn't been there just moments before. A shiny black slug, slowly but surely making its way over the arm of the chair, right next to Tommi.

I couldn't stop myself. I bent over and threw up all over the floor.

Chapter Twenty-five

Tommi started crying. Which brought Dad straight back inside. With every footstep he left little piles of soil on the floor.

Tommi's screams grew louder as the foul smell of my sick rose up to greet me.

I felt very faint and fixed my gaze on one of the patches of earth; I stared and stared, waiting for the moment to pass. The soil was dark brown and grainy, and I could see the pattern from the underneath of Dad's shoe. And as I looked, I saw something else . . . something so small that I wouldn't have noticed it had I not been staring so intently.

A slug was inching its way over the little pile of soil.

I simply opened my mouth and my stomach convulsed again and again until there was nothing left.

'Oh, Effie,' Dad said. 'Let's get you upstairs

into the bath, pet.' He lifted me up in his arms, even though he never, ever carried me any more, and took me upstairs to the bathroom.

He turned on the taps and the room started to fill with steam.

'I'll just sort Tommi out, OK? I'll be right back,' he said, and was gone.

I sat on the toilet, shaking. The warm steam was licking around me, but I felt terribly cold and the nausea would not leave me, even though I was quite empty now. At one point I had to quickly turn and wrench the toilet lid up as my stomach started to churn again, but I brought up only a rank-tasting liquid that burned my throat and mouth and made me feel sicker still.

Dad came back and turned off the taps. He had to really screw the hot one tightly to stop the trickle of water.

I suddenly had a picture in my mind of the bath being left to run so that the water flooded all the way over the white rim and trickled between the floorboards and down the walls to the ground floor. And the water flowed for so long that in the end our house simply floated away and was carried into the loch, disappearing from sight under the murky waters.

But of course, baths don't overflow like that.

There are special little holes near the top, by the taps; the water escapes instead of overflowing. And houses can't float away; they're too heavy. They would sink.

'In you go now, Effie,' Dad said. He sloshed the water around to check the temperature, but as I lowered myself in, it already felt too cold.

I didn't stay in for long. I just wanted to go to sleep and I started to worry that I might doze off; my head might sink under the water and I would never wake up again.

After I got out, I brushed my teeth hard and even gargled with the bright green mouthwash that Dad uses, but I couldn't get rid of the sweet, stale taste in my mouth.

It lingered even after I fell asleep.

I woke when it was still dark and I could still taste it.

The only way to be rid of something is to expel it.

It takes force.

You throw it out of your house with all your might; you spit it out of your mouth until your stomach starts to turn over.

But even when you do all this, things have a way of returning.

Chapter Twenty-six

The next day was a Saturday, and so as soon as I rose, I went to see Finn. I told Dad that I felt better, but I wrapped myself up in layers of clothing and then a coat over the top, even though the sun was shining down brightly and it wasn't that cold outside. I felt I needed to protect myself somehow.

I saw that there was a stain on the living room carpet where I had vomited.

'You can barely see it,' Dad said, and in some lights it was not that visible, but I could still make it out. There was something about the shape of it that made me think of a fat slug. I tried to avoid it, although my eyes were always drawn to it.

Dad didn't seem that fussed about the slugs in Buster's grave. 'There's weirder things than that in the world, Effie. Put it out of your mind.' He was more concerned about the fact that I had been digging up the grave in the first place. He asked me if I thought it had something to do with Mum and whether I wanted to talk to someone. He told me that he could speak to Miss Bell about it; that I could see someone at school.

I wanted to tell him about the slugs creeping onto Mum's binoculars; I wanted to tell him what Old Bill had said about the legend – about the girl who would awaken the monsters . . . And the only detail he had shared about the monsters: that their skin was cold to the touch, and slippery, like the body of a slug.

But Dad looked worried, and I didn't say any more about slugs or legends. Instead I told him that I would think about speaking to someone at school – though in my mind I had decided: I wasn't going to talk to anyone but Finn.

Dad didn't want to hear my theory that Mum hadn't thrown herself in the loch. Just a week earlier, I had come home after school and Dad had been waiting anxiously for me in the living room.

'Dad!' I exclaimed in delight when I saw him there instead of one of the oldies. Then I realized how strange it was. 'Are you OK? Is Tommi all right?'

'Everyone's fine, Effie. Sit down. There's something we need to discuss. Miss Bell rang me today.' I quickly scanned through my memory of the school day but found nothing unusual; I wondered what Dad could possibly want to talk to me about.

'Miss Bell said . . . Miss Bell said that you have been writing about what happened to your mum in class.'

'Umm . . . well, we were set a writing assignment about—'

'Mysteries,' Dad finished for me. 'She read it to me. Effie, why do you continue with this . . . with this . . .' His face started to change, as though the skin was not really his but a mask that was starting to slip off. 'I know how painful it is, but it's time to accept that your mum has gone.'

'But, Dad, we don't know for sure what really happened . . . She might have—' But as I spoke, Dad began to sob. Raw, gasping sobs that shook his whole body.

'I'm sorry, Dad, I'm sorry, I'm sorry.' I would have said anything to stop him crying.

'Effie, we've got to move on. We have to let her go,' he said, his face streaked with tears. From that moment on, I didn't tell anyone other than Finn that I thought Mum might not have thrown herself into the loch that day.

It felt good to be outside again, on my way to see Finn. My spirits rose as soon as I had closed the front door behind me and with every step that took me that little bit further from home.

The sky was the kind of blue that made it look like it would be bouncy if you were able to touch it. I felt myself uncoiling, standing taller, and the tenderness in my stomach drained away.

I always smelled Finn's house before I saw it. Even from the other side of the cherry tree, the smell of something treacly and sweet or the strong, clear scent of a freshly baked loaf would rush to meet me. Later, I wondered how it could have been the same every time. Did Kathleen really bake every single day? But that's how it was.

That morning it was something herby and rich that made my mouth water and reminded me of the dull ache in my tummy.

'Just in time, Effie,' Kathleen said, and turned cheese scones onto a plate next to Finn. He tore his in half, and rich plumes of steam obscured his face, though I could see that it was fixed in a wide grin.

'Right, kids. I'm off to Abiemore now. See you later,' Kathleen said.

I hadn't realized how hungry I was until I smelled those cheese scones; then I remembered that I hadn't eaten last night – and what had happened to my lunch.

'Bye, Mam.' 'Bye, Kathleen,' we mumbled through mouthfuls of hot, floury scone.

'You all right?' Finn said.

'Yes,' I said, because that's what you're programmed to say whenever anyone asks you how you are. And then, 'No,' because it wasn't anyone asking me, it was Finn. 'Fancy a walk?' I asked. I wanted to be outside that day.

We headed for the loch. Without even meaning to, our feet led us there. The loch stretched out before us, wide and open, giving me a sudden feeling of freedom, of release. I breathed more easily, and when I started to tell Finn what had happened the night before, my voice didn't waver.

I told him how I'd seen the earth move; how I'd dug up Buster's grave; about the mass of slugs in the earth; how I alone had noticed the shiny black body of the tiny, tiny one.

Finn's eyes widened as I spoke, and when I got to the part about being sick, his body seemed to hunch over a little in sympathy.

'Are you all right now?' he asked when I'd finished.

'Yes, I think so,' I said. 'I still feel . . . kind of sick. But apart from that, I'm all right.'

'So these slugs . . . They are attracted to the binoculars, your house – in general – *and* Buster's grave. You know what links them all, don't you? I mean, apart from you.'

Finn looked at me levelly. His brown eyes seemed to fill his face; I could only see those eyes, as steady, as sure, as the waters of the loch.

'Your mum.'

Chapter Twenty-seven

I had started to imagine that there were slugs in the room when there were none. I couldn't relax at home. I avoided the garden, where Buster's grave was dark with freshly turned soil, a scar upon the earth.

If the slugs had something to do with Mum, I wanted to find out what; but more than anything, I wanted to be rid of them. And then Finn had a brilliant idea.

'Ask Mrs Daniels to get rid of them,' he suggested. 'A slug's more likely to survive a nuclear disaster than one of her cleaning sprees. It'll be outright war.'

Finn was, of course, quite correct.

The next afternoon, instead of throwing a muttered goodbye over my shoulder as she left the house, I sidled up to her.

'See you then, Effie dear,' she said.

'Bye, Mrs Daniels,' I said, but I did not move from the front door.

'You know you can call me Deidre, dear.'

I'd never call her that.

'Umm.'

'You OK, dear? You look a wee bit pale.' She thrust out a hand and felt my forehead. 'You don't feel hot, though. Is there anything the matter?'

'Umm,' I said again. The oldies always did this to me. They stood right in front of me, and I could never get my words out.

'I wondered if you'd . . . you'd seen any slugs . . .' The words tumbled out of my mouth in a rush, before I could stop myself.

'Slugs?'

'Yes, in the house. I mean, in *our* house.'

'Slugs in this house?' Her eyes narrowed in disgust at the thought of it. 'Why do you ask? Have you seen any?'

'Well . . .'

'You have, haven't you? Whereabouts?' I could almost see Mrs Daniels mentally pulling her sleeves up and reaching for the bleach.

'Well, downstairs. In the kitchen. On the wall in the living room. And on the carpet,' I said, listing the places.

'Oh my goodness, it sounds like a . . . like an infestation,' she pronounced, lingering over every syllable. 'Mind you, I can't say I've ever seen one in this house. I'll have to check with William.'

It took me a moment to realize that she was referring to Old Bill.

'Don't you worry, my dear. If there are slugs here, we will stop them in their tracks, you mark my words. I'll ask Rosemary – she will know what to do. She has a remedy for everything, has Rosemary. Only,' she added quickly, 'don't mention that to your father. I'll just ask her what to do, not to come to the house.'

'Oh,' I said, remembering Dad's reluctance to accept Rosemary Tanner's offer of help. 'Yes, that would be good. Thanks.'

Mrs Daniels strode out of the house, full of purpose, and even after I had shut the front door behind her, I could hear her muttering to herself down the path, 'Slugs! Of all things – slugs!'

The very next day the house was attacked in a blitz of cleaning that left the rooms transformed. Nothing was left untouched. Not the pile of post that Dad had not got round to opening. Not my half-done homework. Every corner was bleached and exposed, and outside, where there were any holes or vents, lay a grey-looking sort of dust.

'It's just a mixture of herbs and a few other things that will send them back where they came from,' Rosemary Tanner told me. 'My da passed it down to me. An old Mivtown recipe. It always worked in our house.' Despite what Mrs Daniels had said, when I got home from school, Rosemary Tanner was there helping her.

'How long have these slugs been getting in?' she asked almost as soon as I walked through the door.

I shrugged. 'A few weeks,' I said, although I remembered the first one very clearly – gliding across the wall outside my parents' bedroom just after Mum had gone missing.

'Only for a matter of weeks then?' she persisted. 'Not longer? Not since, say, Tindlemas?'

I shook my head, although Mum had gone missing shortly after the Christmas holidays had finished, not too long after Tindlemas.

'And have you noticed anything . . . odd about the way they are behaving?'

'Erm, no. Not really,' I said, although my voice wavered.

'Are you sure, girl?' Rosemary Tanner's voice changed suddenly. It reminded me of a dog growling, low and rumbling. But at that moment Mrs Daniels came in, and she quickly said, 'OK, then. Well, that should do it,' in a light sort of way, looking around at the gleaming room with a satisfied sigh.

Mrs Daniels nodded in agreement, dusting her rubber-gloved hands down her apron.

'If you do notice anything, though, Effie, you know you can always tell us . . .' Rosemary Tanner said, stepping closer. 'I mean, you *should* tell us. You don't have to deal with everything on your own.'

She looked over to Mrs Daniels as though to prompt her, and Mrs Daniels's eyes widened in agreement.

'Oh yes, Effie. You can tell us anything – you know you can.'

I nodded, but found myself taking a step backwards.

Rosemary Tanner made sure she was gone before Dad came home, and Mrs Daniels looked at me appraisingly when I didn't mention that she had been there.

That night, as I got ready for bed, I heard Dad exclaiming, 'Look at the bathroom! Effie, have you seen the colour of these tiles?' They were gleaming white – far whiter than the pearly new teeth that had pushed their way through

Tommi's gums; whiter than snowflakes falling from a winter sky.

I nodded. 'That Deidre,' Dad muttered, and I didn't tell him that it was actually Rosemary Tanner who had scrubbed the bathroom.

I fell asleep quickly that night, lulled by the thought that things would get better from now on.

Rosemary Tanner and Mrs Daniels had tackled the house, and I felt sure that under their watch, no slug would dare to cross the threshold.

Sometimes I feel as though I am watching myself from a distance. I walk into a room and I pick something up, but it's not where I mean to be and I'm not holding something I want. Nonetheless it's happening and I can't stop it. I'm just watching it unfold.

It's like what happened by the loch. I couldn't stop myself. It was out of my control.

I couldn't stop myself doing what I did.

Chapter Twenty-eight

The following morning I was washing up the dishes. I hadn't done them last night because I'd been working on my map of Mivtown. I had started adding all the places that Mum had liked: the spot where the bilberry bushes fruited in summer; the place where the old cherry tree grew.

I remembered having a picnic under the tree that looked like a bent arm beckoning. Kathleen and Finn had been there with us, but it was before Tommi was born. There was more food than we could eat, and Finn and I had been practising cartwheels; we kept falling flat on our stomachs, and in the end we gave up.

'You show them how to do it,' Kathleen had told Mum.

'It's been years!' Mum said, laughing.

'Go on!' Kathleen encouraged her.

'Can you do it, Tori?' Finn asked shyly.

'All right.' Mum stood up and brushed the

155

crumbs off her lap. She stood tall, and pushed up on her heels for a second while her arms reached up into the sky. Then she took a deep breath and started cartwheeling down the hill. She did five in quick succession; you couldn't see the gap between one finishing and the next one beginning.

We whooped and cheered and begged her to do some more.

'Go on, Mum,' I said, and in the end she did another lot that left her breathless, her face red and flushed.

'Well, there's no following that,' said Kathleen. 'We'd better get off, Finn. Your daddy's coming home early tonight.'

'Don't go,' I had protested. 'Stay a little longer.'

'We don't have to go just yet, Effie,' Mum said. 'I could teach you how to cartwheel, if you like.'

'I don't want to stay if Finn's going,' I said, and so we didn't. We packed up our things and trailed after them down the hill.

The previous evening I had started to add the tree that looked like an arm to my map, but remembering how the day had ended, I rubbed out the lines.

Now I was running late, trying to clean up and make lunch and leave the house all at once; something was bound to go wrong sooner or later.

That's what happens whenever I try to do more than one thing at a time: if I carry everyone's dinner plate through from the kitchen, I catch my foot on the rug and all the plates come crashing down; when I try to run a bath for Tommi while changing her sheets, the water always gets too hot, and then I have to put cold in, and then I add too much and it's too full and I have to start the whole thing again.

Things need your whole attention; even inanimate things. Or maybe it's just that humans make mistakes when they try to do too many things at once. But sometimes I feel like things want you to notice them.

I filled the washing-up bowl with hot soapy water; at the same time I started to get things out of the fridge to make a sandwich for lunch. There was a knob of stale cheese and an almost empty jar of pickle. That would do. I began scraping off the hard edges of the cheese into the bin, but it was overflowing: a heap of potato peelings sat on top of a mouldy old loaf, threatening to spill over onto the floor. I stopped what I was doing to pull out the heavy bag of rubbish.

Just as I'd tugged the bin bag free, I heard the tell-tale sound of water overflowing, and sure enough, soapy bubbles were now cascading over the side of the washing-up bowl. I considered putting the bag down on the floor to turn off the taps, but it was bulging, rank and ripe; I needed to get it out of the house.

At just that moment, as I stood looking at the roaring water, holding onto that foul-smelling bin, I felt a sharp pain on my right index finger and dropped the bag immediately, spilling the contents onto the floor.

I looked down at my hand – and there was a shiny black slug.

Chapter Twenty-nine

I shook it off my hand and it landed by the pile of rubbish, curling in on itself like a hedgehog.

I spun round to the kitchen sink to wash the cut. Droplets of my blood landed in the water, making red ribbons that danced and then disappeared. I studied the cut: five little pin-pricks that must have been deep – as quickly as the blood was washed away, it came back again.

I turned round and saw that the slug was now moving towards me, leaving a silvery trail in its wake.

Just then I heard someone knocking on the door. Old Bill. Both he and Mrs Daniels have keys, but Old Bill always knocks, while Mrs Daniels just lets herself in.

Without thinking, I knelt down and picked up an empty yoghurt pot that was lying on the floor – one of those big ones that have a proper lid. I quickly scooped the slug into the pot and closed the lid firmly, then dropped it into my school bag as I went to open the door for Old Bill.

'Morning there, Effie,' he said.

'Morning,' I said awkwardly, trying to ignore the pain in my finger. 'I've just had a bit of an accident, I'm afraid. Spilled the rubbish.'

'Oh, right. Leave that to me, Effie. I'll get it cleared up,' and his voice only dropped slightly when he saw the jumbled mix of food and old containers.

'It's a bit of a mess,' I said, bending down to pick up the potato peelings; it was difficult using only one hand – I kept the other hidden from him in my pocket.

'It's nothing,' he said. 'Don't worry about it. You should see my kitchen. You'd better be going, young 'un, or you'll miss your bus.'

I ran all the way down the lane. I could see the bus as I rounded the corner, waiting for me at the edge of the road. The engine was ticking over in the stillness of the street. How could a bus manage to sound cross that I was late? I ran faster still.

When I heard the yoghurt pot knocking against my books, I started to slow down, even though the bus had sounded its horn, a sharp nasal warning. I didn't care, though. I carried my secret carefully onto the bus, avoiding the disapproving glare of Terry, the driver. He muttered something about children today, and pulled away with a jerk before I could find my seat.

'That was close,' Finn said as I slumped down next to him, looping the strap of my bag cautiously over my head. 'I really thought he was going to go without you.'

I didn't reply. My finger was still throbbing and I dug around in my bag for a tissue to staunch the blood.

'How'd it go—' Finn started to say, and then, when he saw the blood, 'Hey, what happened to your finger?'

I looked into his familiar face. I knew it better than my own. His forehead had creased, as it always did when he was worried about something. I'd only seen him do it a few times: when I'd told him about Buster disappearing, and when he found out what had happened to my mum.

'You wouldn't believe me if I told you,' I said, thinking of the shiny little slug sitting on my hand.

'Try me,' he said.

Whispering the events of the morning took the best part of the journey. We had turned down the road of our school by the time I'd finished telling him.

'So it's in the yoghurt pot right this minute?' Finn said in a low voice.

'Yes, in my bag.'

'I hope it's still in there.'

'What do you mean?' I couldn't prevent my voice from rising sharply.

'Well, they must be sharp – their incisors. Just look at your finger.'

I remembered those deep holes and clutched my finger tightly, as if by doing so I could bind the flesh together.

'I just wonder if they are sharp enough to get through plastic,' said Finn.

Chapter Thirty

'All off!' Terry shouted gruffly.

Finn and I were the last off the bus. I held my bag at arm's length all the way along the narrow aisle and down the steps.

I could see our classmates disappearing through the school entrance, their brightly colour-ed jackets engulfed by the stone's dull grey.

'What do we do?' I said to Finn. My arm was beginning to ache.

The bus had driven away now, so there was no one to see us running, hand in hand, in the opposite direction to the school and stopping, breathless, behind an old stone wall.

'We have to see if it's still in the pot,' Finn said.

We both looked at my bag as if it might do something weird like grow two legs and start to dance. But it sat innocently on the grass, keeping its secrets.

Finn found a long stick on the ground; he bent down carefully and lifted the flap. I held my breath. The inside looked dark and ominous, but there was no sign of the creature.

'Don't put your hand in there!' I couldn't help calling out.

'Effie,' Finn chided me. 'You know me better than that.'

Using the stick once more, he lifted the strap so that the whole bag swung off the ground, and then, pinching the base with two fingers, turned it over and emptied it onto the grass in front of us.

'Effie! Finn!' It was the high-pitched call of Miss Bell. We both sank down immediately, our backs to the wall. The contents of my school bag lay half buried in the grass: my pencil case, an old flattened wrapper of a chocolate bar I must have had months ago because I couldn't even remember eating it, the worn cover of my homework diary and, lying not a metre from my feet, the yoghurt pot I'd scooped the creature into. It had pictures of blueberries on its packaging, and as we waited for Miss Bell's calls to fade away, I couldn't take my eyes off them. They were made to look shiny and bright, not like the dull, smoky skin of blueberries at all.

'OK, let's see if we can find it,' Finn said.

The yoghurt pot still had its lid in place, but before I could say anything, Finn had turned the pot over, and there, amidst all the writing, was a small round hole.

It had escaped.

Chapter Thirty-one

We trudged back to school. It was quiet and still, and through the windows I could see the hunched backs of our classmates at their desks.

We'd missed registration and the first lesson had already started. After discovering the hole in the yoghurt pot, we had checked my school bag and the contents on the grass. But there was no sign of the slug.

'You go first,' I said to Finn.

'OK,' he said reluctantly, although we both knew that he was good at this kind of thing. In the face of Miss Bell's astonished expression, Finn described how he'd felt sick when we got off the bus; he'd run off and I had spent all this time persuading him to come back to school.

'Well, you look very well now,' said Miss Bell, taking in his red cheeks and bright eyes.

He stared at her, unblinking, and said, 'I just

needed some fresh air,' and for a moment even I started to believe him.

We barely talked about it for the rest of the day. What was there to say anyway? Having come so close to finding out more about the slugs and whether they had anything to do with the legend, I think we both felt cheated when it disappeared through our fingers.

The monsters from the legend lingered as blurry, shadowy beings at the edge of my mind; as soon as I turned my attention to them, they seemed to disintegrate and disperse like smoke into the night air. The monsters were for chants and taunts between Finn and me, or the sacrifices made by the villagers, not for the clear light of the day; not for the rubbish bag, not for Mum's beloved binoculars.

I couldn't stop thinking about what Old Bill had said about the girl twin touching the monsters in the loch; about the slippery smoothness of their cold skin. Just like a slug's. Were they one and the same? Or was it just a coincidence? Was the legend just for scaring children, as Old Bill thought?

What was galling, we decided, was that we had nothing to show for the events of that morning. I had a cut that could have been made by anything, and a hole in a yoghurt pot. It was like it hadn't really happened at all. We decided not to tell anyone else; to keep it just between us, like the raft and the Tree Cave.

By the time I got home and found that Old Bill had made one of my favourite dinners, dhal and rice, and Tommi had climbed up onto my lap to pat me on the head and say, 'G' girl, Effie,' very solemnly, I was telling myself that maybe it hadn't happened at all. Maybe I'd cut my finger on some rubbish. Maybe.

Perhaps it was better to forget about it and let it fade away completely. Could we have imagined it after all?

I thought about all this, I really did. I hoped that, despite everything, it was not something real and with every day that passed it would fade from me.

Chapter Thirty-two

A few days after the slug escaped I woke up in the middle of the night, my tongue furry and heavy in my mouth, my throat sore.

When we were walking home the previous afternoon, I had felt like I was getting flu. My legs had felt heavy and my head had begun to throb: I had come to a standstill outside the MacGails' cottage and let my head drop.

'Effie, are you all right?' Finn had said, but as he spoke the cottage door swung open and Rosemary Tanner had come striding out.

'What's the matter with you, girl?' she said, and clamped her bony hand to my forehead.

'Nothing,' I said, stepping back. 'Just feel a little woozy.'

'To bed with you, and drink plenty of fluids,' she had snapped, and then she had gestured to Finn and said, 'Go on, take her home! She shouldn't be out.'

Finn had looped his arm through mine and we walked on. I could feel Rosemary Tanner's gaze on us until we were out of sight.

'It was like she was watching us through the window,' Finn remarked once we were out of earshot.

'What's that?'

'Rosemary Tanner. The way she came out so quickly from the MacGails'. It was like she was watching us.'

'Maybe,' I grunted. I didn't feel like speaking any more; my head was pounding.

Once home, I had started to feel worse, but had managed to fall asleep – until the soreness in my throat had woken me.

Now I got out of bed and went downstairs in search of a drink.

I stopped to check on Tommi, who was sleeping soundly, her arms flung above her head, and paused for a moment outside Dad's room. The light was on, but I couldn't hear anything. He must have fallen asleep with his reading lamp on.

I padded softly down the stairs. The house was still and quiet, apart from the wind beating around outside, sending whistles and whispers through any cracks and gaps that it could find in the walls. I stopped to listen to it for a moment.

The windowpanes rattled, which made me jump, but I continued down the stairs, pretending I was someone else; someone who could not possibly be afraid of something like the wind.

It was darker here; no sliver of light shone as it did across the upstairs landing. The curtains had been pulled to against the night and the light of the moon.

For a moment I pictured what I would be doing in a few minutes' time: tucking myself back into bed, sipping a cool drink to soothe my throat. Only the thought that this would be over quite soon allowed me to carry on.

When I reached the kitchen, I instinctively put my hand out to feel for the light switch. I'd lived in this house my whole life and knew every inch of it, even in the pitch-black.

The light flashed on, illuminating the kitchen, and for a second I thought I was in a cave.

A cave that was dark and dank, with walls that glistened with wetness.

But the next moment I saw it for what it truly was.

Every space on the wall.

Every part of the work surface.

The whole length of the ceiling.

It was completely covered.

Covered by the moving bodies of slugs.

Slugs atop slugs atop slugs . . .

All I could see was their blackness. They rode aback another. They squirmed in between the spaces beside each other. They blocked out every part of the kitchen with their shiny, slimy bodies.

I turned to run, but as I did so, one fell off the ceiling, brushing against my cheek. It was cold and wet, and though I rubbed my cheek immediately, I could feel where it had landed; the slime had left its mark upon me. I thought again of the girl twin describing the monsters in the loch, and it made me gasp – a wheezing, terrible breath of fear, pure fear that the monsters were awakening from the depths of the loch.

'Dad! Dad!' I screamed as I ran out of the kitchen, back up the stairs to the narrow beam of light under his door. 'Dad!'

I heard the wind beating against the windowpanes, rattling them as though beating its fist against them, demanding to be let in.

I flung open the bedroom door, taking in the sight of Dad coming to, of my parents' wedding album lying open on the bed, entangled with the sheets.

'Dad! You have to come downstairs. They're in the kitchen. They're everywhere.'

'Who's here?' Dad said, leaping out of bed. 'Someone's in the house?'

'It's . . . it's . . .' I tried to tell him, but he had darted out of the room, clattered down the stairs. 'It's slugs,' I managed to gasp, but he had already gone.

The next moment I heard Dad call up to me. 'It's all right, Effie, no one's here.'

I ran down the stairs again, following Dad's crashing footsteps, and heard Tommi begin to cry; she'd been woken by the noise.

'They're in the kitchen,' I repeated. 'They were just there.'

But before I reached the doorway I could see that I was wrong.

The kitchen was just as it had been earlier that evening. The dishes were on the drying rack, a jug of wilting daffodils stood on the table.

And there was not a slug in sight.

Chapter Thirty-three

'Dad, believe me,' I said for what felt like the hundredth time. 'There were slugs everywhere.'

'But how could that be?' he said again. 'You must have been dreaming, Effie. That's all.'

'I would know if I was dreaming, Dad. I would know it. They were all over the ceiling, over every part of the wall.'

'Well, how could they have disappeared so quickly? Where did they go? It's not a magic trick, is it?'

'I don't know. But they're not normal slugs, Dad.'

'Not normal slugs! Effie, I've heard some tales in the past, but this . . . this . . .'

'They've . . . started to attack us,' I mumbled.

'What do you mean?'

I took a deep breath. 'A slug did this,' I said, and showed Dad the mark on my finger. 'It escaped – Finn and I thought that no one would believe us.'

Dad peered at my finger. There was a mark, but it wasn't very big.

'Effie,' he said slowly. 'Are you saying that you think a slug . . . a slug . . . bit you?'

'Yes. I think they might be something to do with the legend, the monsters, or Mum . . .' I began, and then wished I'd never started because I could see Dad's face begin to fall.

'Effie! Who is filling your head with this nonsense?'

'It's not like that, Dad, and I don't – I don't know anything really. Just what's happened with the slugs and Buster. But the legend—'

'Effie, please stop. You know that the legend is just a silly story that people round here tell because they've got nothing better to do. It's not real. It's just superstitious nonsense.'

'You don't believe me, do you, Dad?'

'Effie,' Dad said, and he took a deep breath too. 'It's not about me believing you or not believing you right now. I think . . . I think . . . that we've all been through a tremendous amount of stress and sadness and it's taking its toll on you. Have you thought any more about speaking to the

person at school . . . about your mum, and all this?'
He waved his arms around, gesturing to what he
thought were my invisible slugs covering the walls
and the ceiling.

'That means you don't.'

'I . . . I . . .' Dad looked around the kitchen as
if the answer was written on the walls. 'I . . . don't
know what to believe.'

We stayed silent for a moment or two, frozen.

'I'd better get Tommi.' I could still hear her
crying upstairs.

'I can do it,' Dad said. 'She'll calm down soon
enough.'

'No – I mean, I'd better get Tommi so we can
leave.'

'Look, Effie, you're tired, I'm tired. Let's just
settle Tommi down and talk about this in the
morning.'

'No, Dad. You don't understand,' I said.

I looked around the room and wondered how
I could prove that we were in danger.

'We can't stay here now.'

I had to spell it out.

'We have to leave.'

Chapter Thirty-four

'You can't wake people up like this,' Dad said, but he didn't stop me from knocking on Finn's dark front door. 'C'mon, Effie. Leave it. Let's go home. We can sleep in the same room, if you like.'

Finn's house stood quiet and sombre; there was no sign that anyone had heard my knocking.

'No, it's not safe there.'

'How do you know it's going to be any safer here?'

'Finn's only had them at his when—' I began, but then thought better of mentioning Mum's binoculars. 'They're not at his house. Only at ours,' I said in the end.

I rapped again, three times in quick succession.

'That's convenient,' Dad said, under his breath.

'What do you mean by that?' I said, but I didn't get the chance to pursue it because at that moment a light came on upstairs; they were awake.

'That's done it.'

I heaved Tommi into a different position on my hip. She had started to nod off as soon as we started walking down the dark path to Finn's house.

I knocked again, and soon after that we heard the soft thuds of footsteps on the stairs.

'Effie. Kev. What's going on?' It was Rob, bleary-eyed. 'Are you OK?'

'Who is it, love?' we heard Kathleen call from inside.

'It's Kev and Effie, and wee Tommi too.'

'Well, don't leave them on the doorstep. They'll catch their death,' said Kathleen. 'Come in, come in, the lot of you. Is everything all right?'

I knew we'd come to the right place.

'We have a favour to ask,' said Dad. 'Well, Effie has a favour to ask,' he corrected himself.

'Sure,' said Kathleen, even though it was two o'clock in the morning. I noticed that she and Rob were wearing matching dressing gowns – blue towelling ones that looked soft and cosy.

'Can we stay here tonight?' I asked.

They looked at each other for a beat.

'If your dad says you can, then sure,' Kathleen said. 'But what's going on? Effie, look at the colour of you. You look as white as a sheet.'

'I've been overruled,' Dad said. 'If Effie wants to stay here, then Effie will stay here.'

Kathleen and Rob exchanged another look. I suppose when you've been a couple for as long as they have, you don't need words to understand each other.

'Dad, you should stay here too,' I said. 'It's not safe in the house.'

'What's going on here?' Rob said.

'Ask Effie.' Dad turned away from us.

'Mum?' came Finn's voice down the stairs.

'It's all right, love,' Kathleen said. 'Effie's here. They're having some . . . they're having some trouble.'

'Effie?' I heard Finn muttering to himself and the soft plodding of his steps down the stairs.

'Hi, Finn,' I said. 'They were everywhere – they covered the kitchen completely.'

'Oh!' Finn's mouth made a wide O of astonishment. 'Are you OK?'

'Yes,' I said quickly. 'But . . .' and I found myself suddenly starting to cry. I swallowed hard a few times to stop myself.

'Are they still there?'

'No, they just vanished. As soon as Dad came down.'

Suddenly I noticed all three adults watching us, listening in.

'Will someone please explain what's going on?' said Kathleen.

'It's not going to sound like it makes much sense,' Finn started, 'but Effie and I have reason to believe that some creatures are trying to attack her.'

'What do you mean, *creatures*?' Rob said.

Dad couldn't stop himself: 'Slugs. They think slugs are attacking them. From the bloody legend of Mivtown!'

'Not *us*,' Finn said carefully. 'It's only Effie. Not me.'

'Finn?' said Kathleen. 'I don't understand. Slugs? The legend?'

'We don't know for sure if it's connected to the legend, but the monsters have the same sort of skin as slugs and so we think it is,' Finn said. 'They look like slugs, but they're not. And they're attracted to certain things. And we just found out yesterday that they can draw blood.'

I was glad Finn was there. He had a way of explaining things that made them sound reasonable and sane.

When I spoke, my words had the opposite effect.

Chapter Thirty-five

'They don't believe us,' came Finn's voice in the darkness, once Kathleen had kissed us both on the forehead and turned off the light.

Dad had guffawed throughout our explanations. 'Where are you kids getting this claptrap from?' he had shouted.

Kathleen and Rob were quieter. Rob had scratched his head quizzically and kept stopping himself from saying anything. Kathleen just seemed sad: she looked first at Finn and then at me, and then back at Finn again.

'I think your mum does . . . a little,' I said now.

'Maybe. I think she wants to.'

'That's worth something.'

Finn's breathing gradually turned heavier and deeper. Soon I heard light, wispy snores, and as he slept, I stole from my bed and tiptoed out into the warm glow of the landing.

First I checked on Tommi. She was flat out,

her arms and legs sticking out at her sides. I spent a few minutes listening to the steady rhythm of her breathing, then carefully closed the door so it didn't make a sound.

From the landing I could hear our parents' voices through the slightly open living-room door, but not what they were saying. I silently went down a few steps so I was close enough to hear them, and perched there, ready to flee if the door started to swing open.

I imagined them all taking sips of amber whisky from their glasses.

'It's been a long, long time since they did it,' I heard Kathleen say.

And then Rob said something: something about slugs.

I crept further down the stairs.

Dad was speaking now – something about monsters, I think, but he was mumbling.

'That's the thing,' Kathleen said. 'You saw their faces. It doesn't seem to me like they're lying.'

I was in the hall now, only steps away from the living room. 'They believe in what they're saying so much that they don't think they're lying any more,' Dad said. 'They've forgotten about the part where they made it all up.'

'It's not like before,' Kathleen insisted. 'When

it happened before, I could see it in Finn's face: he'd be expecting you. It wasn't like that tonight; he was as surprised as we were.'

What did they mean by *before*? What had happened before this? I shivered in my pyjamas, but was unable to prise myself away.

'I suppose you have a point, love,' said Rob. 'Finn did seem pretty out of it. Remember the first time it happened? He kept begging us to stay up just a little longer. We didn't know what had got into him – normally he's out like a light. He kept saying, *Please, just five more minutes, five more minutes.* And then we heard the knock on the door.'

'God, Tori was beside herself,' said Dad. 'She tried everything. Anything to settle her down. But no, Effie wouldn't have it. She wouldn't stop until she was marching over to your house in her slippers and dressing gown. She kept saying, *It's not safe here – we have to go to Finn's*, over and over until she wore us out.'

'What was it she said had happened? I've forgotten now,' asked Rob.

'A ghost in her cupboard tried to eat her.'

'And they couldn't get in here because of the force field,' Rob said, remembering.

'Her screams – I thought they would raise the whole village. As soon as we suggested something – anything other than sleeping here – she'd start to scream. It was easiest just to bring her round here for the night.'

'You know, I'd forgotten how bad it was. Effie's such a grand little lass now. I'd forgotten how wilful she could be,' said Rob.

'Wilful? Stubborn, more like,' said Dad. 'And determined. Tori was in such a state, saying what a rotten mother she must be. That Rosemary didn't help when she heard what had been happening. She kept coming round at bedtime, dropping in to get a front-row seat. In the end Tori just stopped answering the door to her. But I told Tori that she should stop blaming herself. She should look at the little girl we'd created: we'd never need to worry about her future – she knew exactly what to do to get her own way. She wouldn't let anybody or anything stop her.'

I swallowed hard. There was a mirror in Finn's hallway, an old-fashioned thing set into a funny wooden dresser, so when I looked up I could see my reflection. Was I this person they were describing? I looked at myself: the hazel-brown eyes, the fringe hanging down over my forehead. The picture that Dad was painting was of someone monstrous, someone spoiled and horrible, someone I wouldn't like. I started to tiptoe back up the stairs, but I could still hear the voices. I wished I could make them stop.

'It wasn't an easy time,' Kathleen said. I was glad that she had spoken. I hoped that she didn't see me like this; that maybe she saw something else. 'I think it got to Effie.'

'What do you mean by that?' Dad said, in a dangerously quiet voice.

'Oh, nothing,' she said lightly. 'It's just that, you know, we all know it's not easy being a parent.'

'No, I don't know. What do you mean?'

'Nothing, Kev, nothing.'

'You must have meant something or you wouldn't have said it.' I could almost hear the whisky in Dad's voice, thick and dangerous, rising like a tall wave in the sea.

'Oh, Kev. You knew about it – we all did . . . Tori, she was . . . I mean, I loved her to pieces, but she was very protective of Effie.'

'Kathy,' said Rob, like a warning.

'Are you saying it was Tori's fault? That it was Tori who drove her to make up stories to come over here?'

'No, not at all. I just meant it's hard, you know. And then that business with Rosemary . . . I'm just saying it was hard. For everyone. And I can't imagine how Tori must have been feeling last year – I can't imagine.'

There was a heartbeat of heavy silence. I could imagine Dad staring into the distance, Kathleen glancing nervously at him.

'I'd better be off,' said Dad. I heard the chair creak and shift as he stood.

I quickly darted up the rest of the stairs, as lightly as I could.

'Kev, don't leave like this,' said Rob, following Dad into the hall. 'We stopped being friends when all that happened. Like Kath said, it's not easy being a parent . . . I know Effie's carrying on the way she did must have been hard. We've never spoken of it before tonight, but maybe now's the time—'

'You don't know anything about it.' The way Dad spoke made me think he was about to cry. With that he left, and by the time I heard the front door close behind him, I was standing outside Finn's bedroom, my hand resting on the cold brass doorknob.

I was about to turn it when I heard Rob's voice float up to me.

'You know what I was going to say?' he said to Kathleen. 'That life's too short to lose a friend.'

Then there was only the sound of Dad's footsteps disappearing down the path.

Chapter Thirty-six

'Effie, love,' said Kathleen. 'It's time for school.'

I coaxed my heavy limbs from my bed on the floor and felt a pain reach sharp fingers all the way up to my temples as I sat up. The conversation I had overheard last night wove its way through my mind, not letting me forget it.

'Where's Tommi?' Usually what wakes me first is the sound of her calling for me.

'Your dad's been over to get her. Old Bill's looking after her today; he was able to start early.'

'OK,' I said, defeated. I wouldn't be able to protect Tommi if it was only Finn and me who believed the slugs were a danger.

Dad had brought round a bag of clothes for me, but he'd packed my old school jumper that was too small for me. I felt uncomfortable and restricted in it, as tightly bandaged as a mummy, but there was a cold wind, so I had no choice but to wear it. On top of the bag I found a brown envelope with my name on it, but the writing was not Dad's.

'What's this?' I asked Kathleen.

'Oh, it's nothing,' she said. 'Rosemary Tanner brought it round for you. She said that she saw you weren't well in the lane yesterday – it's tea to make you better. Bill told her that you were here – she insisted on leaving it for you. You don't have to drink it; in fact, you'd better not. I have no idea what Rosemary puts into those remedies of hers.'

'I don't think I will,' I said, looking at the grey, dust-like powder that was inside.

'Here – I'll make you a ginger, honey and lemon instead,' Kathleen said; she took the envelope and threw it away.

'What shall we do?' I asked Finn as the school bus set off. Mivtown disappeared behind us, and for an uncanny moment the village seemed stagnant, waiting until our return.

'We could show them the slugs on the binoculars,' Finn suggested. 'That's something they can see in front of them.'

'But Dad didn't think that there was anything wrong with Buster's grave; he didn't reckon it was that strange. Maybe they won't think the slugs on Mum's binoculars are that strange either. But how can they not sense it? How can they not see that something's wrong?'

'Maybe they don't want to,' Finn said.

'I overheard our parents talking last night,' I said. 'After you went to sleep I snuck downstairs.'

'What did they say?'

'Just that they didn't believe us,' I said, not wanting to repeat what Dad had said about me. 'But they said something about Rosemary Tanner. About Mum and Rosemary Tanner. Do you know anything about that?'

'No.' Finn shrugged. 'Apart from – well, they didn't seem to like each other.'

I paused, trying to think of the times they had spent together, and found that I couldn't see them side by side in my head.

'Mum never said it out loud, but I don't think she liked Rosemary Tanner – or any of the oldies – that much really,' I said. 'And Dad doesn't want her in the house. I think that was because of Mum not liking her.'

'Your mum avoided her,' Finn said. 'People don't like the way she goes on about the legend. I don't think anyone really believes in it but Rosemary Tanner.'

'But what about the other oldies? They must do.'

'Maybe not in the same way,' Finn mused. 'Like Old Bill said, the legend is about keeping children away from the water. He doesn't really think there are monsters in there.'

'I don't know . . . he also said that he couldn't get them out of his head. Maybe there's something he didn't want to admit to us. Perhaps the oldies know more than we think, especially Rosemary Tanner. She was asking me about the slugs – when they turned up and that kind of thing. She might think they are like the description the girl twin gave – the feel of them . . .'

'Yes,' Finn agreed.

'And maybe it's time to ask your mum about things too. About when we were born.'

The school day passed slowly, as things do when you are impatient for them to end; the tiredness that hung over me like a cloud didn't help.

'There isn't one example of this in this poem, there are many . . .' Miss Bell's voice had lulled me into a semi-conscious state. Somewhere between wakefulness and light dozing.

'Here's one: *Did gyre and gimble* . . . Second line down.' I felt my head begin to nod – I couldn't help myself.

'Who can give me another?'

Miss Bell's question sounded foggy and far away. 'Effie?'

It wasn't her voice saying my name that woke me but the sharp kick that Finn had delivered under the table.

'Umm . . . pardon?' I said. I looked around, startled, and blinked my eyes open. A couple of children sniggered.

'Don't be so rude, Effie Waters,' Miss Bell said. She fixed me with a stare. 'It doesn't suit you.'

I really hadn't meant to be rude – although I supposed that didn't matter because Miss Bell thought I had.

'Sorry, miss.'

'Now that we have your attention, Effie, perhaps you could point us in the direction of an example of Lewis Carroll using nonsense words to create atmosphere . . .'

I looked down at the page. The words swam in front of my eyes as I tried to understand what Miss Bell was asking me. At times like this Finn and I always agreed that you should concentrate on looking at whatever it is you're asked about, then pick the first thing you see.

I scrunched up my face as if I were thinking very hard. After a moment or two I chose a word from the very top of the page.

'*Slithy?*' I ventured.

Miss Bell looked taken aback. 'Yes, slithy,' she said. She gave me an appraising look. 'What does that make you think of?'

I sighed, but only on the inside. 'It makes me think of . . . of . . .' and I scrunched up my face once more and bent over to study the poem. I concentrated on the word 'slithy' so much that it stopped looking like a word at all – it was just little black lines and squiggles on the white page.

'*Slithy,*' Miss Bell repeated slowly, letting the word slide off her tongue.

'Slugs,' I said, sitting back up. Finn straightened in his chair as I said it. 'It makes me think of slugs.'

'Yes, I see what you mean,' Miss Bell said. 'I suspect slugs are rather slithy too. Good.'

The slugs weren't only in our house now. They were in my head.

Chapter Thirty-seven

When I got home from school, I overheard Old Bill talking on the phone. I had slipped in through the back because I'd stepped in a large puddle on the lane and didn't want to tread mud through the house.

'Listen – listen to me,' he said, and there was a note of urgency in his voice that I had not heard before. 'We made the offering, didn't we? We did the Tindlemas. What's it got to do with her?'

Just then, Tommi saw that I'd snuck into the kitchen and started shouting for me. I heard Old Bill quickly hang up the phone; when he came through to greet me, I noticed that he looked a little flustered and his cheeks were flushed.

'Effie,' he said. 'Didn't hear you come in.' Was I imagining that he was looking at me anxiously?

'Just had muddy shoes,' I said.

'Well, I'll get going now. Your dinner's in the pot on the stove. Just needs warming through.'

'Thanks,' I said, and for a moment I thought of asking him if he knew anything else about the legend. But something stopped me. 'Bye then.'

'Cheerio.' For a second I thought Old Bill was going to say something more too, but then he turned and left me alone with Tommi – and the sinking feeling that perhaps he was not someone we could trust after all.

It was harder than I'd expected to ask Kathleen about what had happened when we were born, and to find out what Rosemary Tanner thought about the slugs.

I rarely saw Rosemary Tanner and I didn't want to venture to her cottage to ask her outright. I decided to wait until she was round at ours again, or until I passed her in the village.

Every time I tried to talk to Kathleen, something stopped me. Sometimes it was me: the words were on my tongue, but there they stayed, heavy and stubborn, refusing to budge. Other times, I opened my mouth to speak, and then Finn or Rob would come in, unsettling me; I wanted to ask Kathleen when we were alone.

Did she wonder why I was hanging around with her rather than with Finn, who was looking through Mum's binoculars from his bedroom window? She didn't remark on it. She sat sewing a quilt for the Lambs' baby, Colan, and the movement of her hands soothed me almost into a trance. Then Rob would come in from work, and I had missed my chance once again.

'It's looking great, love,' he remarked, looking at the colourful patchwork of squares on her lap, growing slowly, piece by piece.

'Yes,' I agreed, and then, thinking aloud, 'Maybe you could make one for Tommi?'

'Of course,' Kathleen replied, beaming. 'I'd love to. You could help me if you wanted. I could teach you . . .'

'Oh, I don't think I could—'

'It's not difficult. Really. Just takes time. And practice. Remember, Rob, when I was starting out? I made some right humdingers. But then I got better.'

'Aye, that's right,' said Rob. 'There was a time when every female in Mivtown was wearing a Kathleen Original.'

'Even my mum?' I asked.

'Aye. Even your mum. Didn't you make Tori that maternity dress with the little flowers on, Kath? You had matching ones.'

'Yes,' she said softly – at the same time as I said, 'I know that dress! It's my favourite!'

She smiled over at me. I thought of that dress now: buried several feet under the ground, out of sight, and for the first time I wished I hadn't put it in Mum's coffin.

'I liked the flowers,' I said awkwardly.

'Yes, your mum chose the material. She liked the flowers too. She said they reminded her of the plant that grows at the edge of the loch.'

'Bladderwort,' I said, the name appearing on my lips like a conjuring trick. 'That's what it's called.'

Kathleen sat up quickly, as though a thought had just occurred to her. 'I think I still have some! I'm sure I came across a bit when I was sorting through my fabric for Colan's quilt. Would you like it?'

'Yes,' I said, suddenly feeling shy.

Kathleen dug around in the trunk beside her chair and pulled out one of the scraps. It was only a small piece, but it felt silky; maybe a little worn, but all the better for it because it had lost its stiff edge of newness.

I stuffed the fabric into my pocket so I wouldn't forget it, and all afternoon I kept delving into its soft, silky folds to check that it was still there.

That night I fingered the piece of flowered

fabric as I lay in bed. It was as soft and reassuring as the old yellow baby blanket that Tommi still liked to sleep with.

When I slept, I dreamed of Mum. She was at the loch, walking on the water towards me, and even though I knew that this was impossible, I didn't think it was weird, I thought it was normal. Dreams change the rules of what you can accept.

Her hair was far longer than it had ever been when she was alive. It hung all the way down her back and looked as silvery as the water itself, but it was her skin that was really remarkable: it was etched with the same flower print as the fabric – the webbed leaves and yellow, trumpet-like flowers of the bladderwort – like a tattoo . . . Although it didn't look like it had been drawn on like a tattoo; it looked like it was part of her.

Every part of her was covered in the tiny flowers and leaves – the soft skin of her eyelids right down to her little toes.

I didn't say, 'Mum' when I saw her. I just said, 'Tori Waters,' as if she and I were strangers to each other, meeting for the first time.

Then she said: 'Effie Waters.'

And I woke up.

This morning I woke from a dream where I was in the water again. The sky turned black, just as it did before, but this time there's not Da's arm to rescue me, and I wake at the exact moment when I start to sink down.

It takes me a moment to remember who I am, where I am, how old I am now. I'm no longer a child.

That's when I felt the slug on my arm. It felt quite terrible against my skin. Such coldness, like death itself. I pulled it off. I couldn't bear to have it touch me.

It made me think only one thing.

It has begun . . . And I would do anything to stop it.

Chapter Thirty-eight

After my dream about Mum I couldn't get back to sleep.

I spent a few moments telling myself that it wasn't real, but the image lived on in my mind; I couldn't shake it. Mum's face was still indelibly etched upon me.

I dragged my sleep-heavy body out of bed. I stumbled at first, my limbs protesting, but then I got my balance and took unsteady steps towards my window to look out at the loch.

You could barely see it in the darkness. Each time the moon's white face appeared from behind a cloud, the light caught the ripples in the water. But otherwise you wouldn't have known it was there. I could imagine it, though, lying in wait like a slippery secret. Black and full of distorted reflections. So dark that you could never see the bottom.

There was no sign of Mum walking on the water, though, that was for sure.

'There's nothing there,' I said out loud, and by now I was fully awake.

The house was silent, apart from the occasional drips from the bathroom tap, which always leaked no matter how tightly you turned it. I looked in on Tommi, who was sound asleep in a warm bundle. I checked the room for slugs, and finding none, settled back into my bed, seeking out the warmth of my duvet but finding it cold and unwelcoming.

I envied Tommi's ignorance; if she woke up, she expected everyone else to as well. I would like to have woken Dad or Tommi rather than sitting by myself, my feet cold on the floorboards. I no longer believed that I was at the centre of things, and I knew better than to wake Dad, who needed to work tomorrow, or Tommi, who would get upset because she wouldn't understand.

In the end I switched on my lamp rather than sitting in the darkness, and after blinking in the golden beam I pulled the duvet around me once more, and reached for my book.

I suddenly realized that there was something missing from my bedside table . . . Something had gone, but I couldn't say what. I stared at it for a few minutes, trying to play Spot the Difference against a blurry image in my head. What was it?

The book was where I always left it, its ragged bookmark still sitting in the page I'd last read; my alarm clock said 3:10 in bright red digits; the lamp stood in the corner. Next to the clock were a couple of hairbands, as there always were, and my wristwatch, face up.

I couldn't tell you what was missing, but I knew, with the cold chill of certainty, that someone had stolen into my bedroom that night and had taken something from me.

Chapter Thirty-nine

'If you don't know what it is, then it can't be that important,' Finn said when I told him.

'It is,' I insisted. 'It doesn't matter that I don't know what it is. The point is, someone got into our house, came into my bedroom and took it from right next to where I was sleeping.'

'But how do you know it was there when you don't remember what it was?' Sometimes Finn is frighteningly logical.

'I know it was something . . . something important.' The idea was racing round and round my head, but each time I thought I was close to it, it sped up and disappeared round the corner, just out of my grasp.

'Try not to think about it. It'll probably come to you then.'

'OK. Let's talk about something else.'

'So you didn't ask my mum in the end?'

'No – I was about to, but your dad came home and— Finn!' I said. 'That's what went missing! The fabric!' I thought of the tiny scrap that Kathleen had given me. For a moment I'd had a piece of Mum that I could hold in my hand, and now it was gone.

'What?'

'From my bedside table!'

When Finn's puzzled expression didn't change, I explained: 'Your mum gave me an old piece of fabric yesterday. The same material as my mum's dress – the flowered one. That's what's missing.'

'But why would anyone take an old bit of fabric from your bedroom?'

'Beats me,' I said.

'Your dad!' he guessed. 'I bet he came in to check on you and saw the fabric. He probably just wanted to remember your mum or something.'

'I don't know, Finn. I don't think Dad checks up on me any more.'

'Oh, sure he does. Mine does all the time. I'm always having to pretend I'm asleep.'

'Maybe. I'll ask him.' I paused, trying to imagine Dad creeping into my room, trying not to wake me. 'What if it's not him?'

'Let's check your bedroom . . . A bit of fabric could easily have slipped down or floated off the table. I bet we find it under your bed or something.'

'Maybe,' I said.

But I didn't believe it for a second.

Chapter Forty

Dad looked at me blankly that evening when I asked him if he had come into my room last night.

'What do you mean by that, Effie?' were his exact words.

'Erm, I just wondered if you'd taken anything . . .'

Dad frowned.

'I wouldn't mind if you did,' I said quickly.

'Like what?' he asked.

I didn't want to tell him about the fabric unless I had to; there was no point in bringing Mum up if he didn't know what I was talking about.

'It's just that I lost something . . . You know when you lose something but you can't remember what it is? It's like that.'

'Not really, Effie. But I didn't go into your room last night, if that helps.'

'Not once?'

'No, not even once.'

'OK, thanks, Dad,' I said, walking away. I suddenly remembered what Finn had said about his dad checking on him when he was meant to be asleep. I turned round again.

'Dad, do you ever check on me still? You know – when I'm sleeping? I don't mean last night; I mean, just generally. Like we check on Tommi. To see if she's OK.'

Dad scratched his beard and looked vaguely troubled – as if it was the first time he'd ever thought about it.

'No, not now you're a big girl, Effie,' he said, but he looked worried.

I turned away again – quickly because tears were pricking behind my eyes. It was so silly. I really didn't care if Dad checked on me or not.

'Hope you find it, Effie,' he said.

'What?' I said, blinking away my tears so he wouldn't notice them.

'Whatever it is you're looking for.'

'Oh, yes,' I said. 'Me too.'

After that I rang Finn and asked him to come round. I didn't want to check my bedroom on my own. I was afraid of what I might find.

'See anything?' Finn asked.

I was flat on my stomach, shining a torch into the dark space under my bed to see what was there.

'Nothing yet,' I said. I guided the torch beam around the shadows, checking each item.

'If it had just fallen down, it wouldn't be that far under,' Finn said. His voice sounded muffled, as if he was calling into a cave rather than just under the bed.

'*Here* are all my hairbands,' I muttered. They were clogged with dust; together, they looked like the body of a fat spider squatting on its web.

I started to shuffle sideways, throwing the beam of light this way and that as I moved.

'Hold on,' I said. I'd seen something in the corner. I moved a little further in and directed the torch towards the spot.

There, lying on the carpet, was a scrap of material, so tiny that I could only make out a section of one of the printed flowers; the arches of a few petals and the curve of its stem. It was as small as the tip of my little finger; I didn't dare breathe as it lay in the palm of my hand in case it blew away. It was pure luck that I'd managed to spot it at all.

'I've got something,' I said.

'The material?'

'Sort of.'

'Come out, then,' said Finn impatiently.

'Coming,' I said. But I didn't move.

I pointed the torch at the small scrap. Part of me didn't believe it was sitting innocently on my palm, as delicate as a feather or a dandelion seed that could be carried off by a breeze at any moment. It might vanish when I brought it out from under the bed; disintegrate into nothing.

'C'mon, Effie,' Finn said.

'Coming,' I said again. 'Coming. I just need to see if there's any more.'

I scrambled further into the dark corner, my fist tightly clenched over the scrap of fabric, which made it hard to move as I was holding the torch in my other hand and couldn't let go of either.

At one point I dropped it – the torch, I mean – and as I reached out to pick it up, I felt my fingers brush against something.

Something wet. Something cold.

Chapter Forty-one

I withdrew my hand instantly, as you do when you feel something unexpected.

'Effie?'

'There's something under here,' I said in a whisper.

'What?' Finn said.

'Something wet.'

He paused for a few seconds. 'You think it's one of them?'

'Yes,' I said.

'You've got the torch, though – shine it on it.'

'I can't,' I said. 'I dropped it and the thing was right by it.'

'Did you see it?'

'No, I just felt it.'

'It might not be one,' said Finn. 'Just pick up the torch and have a look.'

I was frozen, rigid; I couldn't see how I was

going to get my hand or any part of me to move again.

'C'mon, Effie,' Finn said. 'You can do it.'

I whispered to myself: '*Effie, you can do it.*'

And then, '*Do it, Effie. Do it. Three . . . two . . . one . . .*'

'Effie? Do you want me to come?'

'No,' I said sharply. I didn't want to put Finn in danger. From the moment my hand came into contact with the cold, slippery surface, I'd felt it. Danger. I reached out for the torch, walking my fingers over its ridges, and when I felt nothing but plastic casing, I closed my fingers around it. It was solid, reassuring and familiar.

I shone the light around slowly – and that's when I saw it.

It was a photograph frame; one of those ornate, golden swirly ones. It was choked with dust – I poked out great matted clumps of the stuff. It must have been lying there for a long time.

The picture was of Mum holding me as a baby. I was bundled up in my yellow blanket, wearing a little white hat, looking impossibly small in her arms. You couldn't really see Mum's face because she was gazing down at me. It looked like she was trying to take a photograph of my face, she was studying it so intently.

All in a rush, I felt something like an ache, something like happiness settle in my chest. Up until then I had never known that this picture existed.

I let my hand brush over the cool glass . . . *That* was what I had felt in the darkness. It wasn't a slug after all, just the glass of the photo frame. Nothing dangerous.

'Look what I found,' I said, brandishing the photograph at Finn.

He blew the dust off and then pulled the sleeve of his jumper over his fist to rub away the cloudy trails of grime that remained. 'It's you.'

'And this . . .' I unfolded my hand to reveal the tiny scrap of fabric I'd found.

'What is it?'

'It's part of the material that I had last night. That Mum's dress was made of.'

'It's tiny! No wonder you lost it!'

'No, this isn't it, this is just part of it. The piece I had was bigger.'

'Where's the rest of it?'

'Good question.'

'And how did this bit get snipped off?'

'Who knows?' I said. 'It's just another thing to add to all the other stuff we can't explain.'

'I suppose,' said Finn, rising to the challenge,

'it could have been from when my mum made your mum's dress. Maybe they cut it out in your bedroom. I mean, before it was your bedroom.'

'It's a good idea, but there's one problem with that.'

'What?'

'Well, look at it – it's not dusty enough. Everything else under there is caked in dust.'

'Hmm,' said Finn. 'In that case . . . I . . . I have no idea how it ended up there.'

'C'mon, Finn,' I said. 'You can do better than that.' I wasn't used to him not working things out. I was the one who usually gave up. 'It was on my bedside table when I fell asleep. When I wake up about five hours later, it's gone, and all we can find is part of the material under my bed. Dad hasn't been in here. Tommi was asleep.'

'OK,' said Finn. 'Let's work backwards. Whatever or whoever put the scrap there had to be small enough to get under your bed.'

'Right, so they could be as big as me or as small as . . . as small as a . . .'

Finn looked me in the eye, and I knew without him saying a word that we were thinking the same thing.

As small as a slug.

Chapter Forty-two

It didn't make any sense.

But then, nothing over the last few weeks had made much sense.

I saved that tiny last scrap of fabric, though. I tucked it carefully into my copy of *The Velveteen Rabbit* – at the place where the fairy comes down and makes the rabbit real. I was glad to have found the photograph of me, newly born, wrapped in Mum's arms. I carved out a space for it on my bookshelf, where it sat snugly in between the spines of the old picture books I'd read when I was little and had saved for Tommi.

'That's a lovely photo of you and your mum,' Old Bill said to me absent-mindedly one day.

'What photo?' I said, my ears spiking.

'Oh, the one in your bedroom. I saw it when I was up there . . . dusting.'

I didn't answer, although I doubted Old Bill had ever done any dusting in our house. Again, I felt that I couldn't trust him any more, that he wasn't telling us the whole truth. I wondered aloud to Finn whether he might have had something to do with Mum going.

'Old Bill?' he said, slightly doubtfully.

'He's hiding something,' I said. 'It might be to do with Mum.'

'What about Rosemary Tanner? What did she say?'

I'd finally managed to ask her about the slug when I had come home to find her in the house with Mrs Daniels and Tommi.

'Effie, dear.' She'd stood up from the kitchen table when she saw me, and I noticed that she was still wearing muddy boots. 'Deidre's just changing young Tommi upstairs. She got a wee bit muddy on our walk.'

She saw me glance down at her boots and exclaimed, 'Well, look what I've gone and done!'

She stomped towards the back door, trailing mud, and struggled to take her boots off.

'There,' she said finally. When she returned, some of her hair had come loose and hung greasily down the side of her face.

'I'll just mop this lot up. Won't take a jiffy,' she said, and went to get the mop and bucket from under the stairs. There was a crash and a bang as she rummaged around in the cupboard, but when she returned, she was empty-handed. She went and stood stiffly by the sink.

'Don't worry about mopping,' I said unnecessarily, unsure what to say or where to look.

Rosemary broke the silence: 'I hear you haven't seen the end of the slugs yet?'

I looked up sharply. 'Um, no.'

'Deidre told me.'

'Oh,' I said.

'We found a few here this morning actually. Seems like they are spreading. We had a good go at the floors this morning – before I muddied them again. And we put down another load of Da's remedy.'

Rosemary stamped down hard on the tiles, grinding her foot into the floor. 'Got you!' she said.

'Another one!' she exclaimed, incredulous. 'I don't know where they're coming from.'

'Did any get onto Tommi?' I asked.

'Lord, no,' she said in astonishment. 'We wouldn't let them near her, don't you worry.'

'OK, good.'

'We'll always keep her safe, Effie,' Rosemary Tanner said meaningfully. She reached out for her black book and hugged it to her.

'I know,' I said. 'It's just that the slugs—'

'What about them?'

'Well, I think they can hurt you.'

'What makes you think that?'

I raised my finger slowly to show her the mark the slug had left.

Rosemary Tanner put her hand to her mouth with a gasp. 'A slug did that to you?' she asked.

I nodded.

'When did that happen?'

'Just a few days ago.'

'No!'

After all this time, finally someone believed me.

'I'm very sorry to hear that,' Rosemary Tanner said gravely.

The expression of shock on her face had now changed to something different.

A look of acceptance. And of resolution.

Chapter Forty-three

We were working on the raft in the Tree Cave when it happened.

Finn and I had finally finished nailing down the planks.

'We need to see if it floats before we do anything else,' Finn said. I had finished sanding the paddle and there was nothing more to do.

'Let's go for a walk by the loch,' he suggested.

'What time is it?'

'It's twelve fifteen. We've just missed her.'

Having spent a lot of time in the Tree Cave, we had become familiar with Rosemary Tanner's routine: we knew that she did three rounds of the loch each day – one at nine, the next at midday and the last at four in the afternoon. We had learned not to enter or leave the Tree Cave at those times; we knew that we might bump into Rosemary Tanner and give away our hidey-hole.

The loch looked grey and peaceful that day.

The sun was shining on it; glints were caught on the surface like diamonds sparking in the light. For the first time in ages I remembered how beautiful it was.

'Look at it, Finn!' I couldn't help exclaiming.

The sun's rays skipped across the surface, lighting it up.

'On a day like this you wouldn't think there was any such thing as monsters,' I continued, feeling peaceful when I looked at the water, rather than full of fear of what it might contain.

'I suppose so,' said Finn. 'But think of the bladderwort – looks can be deceiving.' I remembered that the bladderwort was carnivorous; it captured its prey by snapping shut while the victim was distracted by its pretty yellow flower.

'I don't think there are really monsters in there,' I said, looking out over the sparkling water, and took a step closer to the edge. 'Not really. What was it Old Bill said? That it was a story to keep children safe. That's all the legend is.'

'What are you doing, Effie?' Finn said suddenly.

I had kicked off my boots and started to unpeel my socks.

'I'm going to show you,' I said, 'how unafraid I am of it all.' I sounded stronger than I felt, but with every move I became more in control; I began to feel something like freedom. Freedom from the legend, freedom from myself.

'Effie, don't do it,' Finn said, his voice rising with worry.

'Honestly, Finn,' I said. 'There's nothing to worry about.'

Rolling my jeans up to my knees, I took a step into the water. It was freezing, but I kept stepping forward. Something told me to keep moving.

'See? There's nothing to worry about,' I said again, although my teeth chattered violently as I spoke.

I continued to paddle, with Finn looking on anxiously.

'Don't go too far, Effie,' he kept saying, and I could feel his eyes on me.

'I won't,' I promised.

Suddenly I heard a scream from the other side of the loch. It was high-pitched and ragged.

'What was that?'

Now that it had died away, I wondered if it was human or if it could have been an eagle flying overhead.

'Come out now,' Finn said. 'Come out. Come on, you've proved your point.'

'All right, all right,' I said, and I waded back towards him.

My jeans had got wet and were beginning to feel heavy. When I reached the bank, I climbed out carefully. My feet had been numb, but they started to hurt when I got out of the water.

'Very funny,' I said, looking around. 'You can give them back now.'

'Give what back?'

'My boots,' I said. 'They were just here.' I pointed to the patch of grass by a large rock; I clearly remembered leaving them there.

'I haven't touched them, I swear.'

'Come on, Finn. Hand 'em over now. My feet are freezing.'

'Honestly, Effie, I haven't got them. I promise.'

We went round and round like this in circles – until finally Finn, red in the face, swore on Kathleen and Rob's lives that he didn't have them. He wasn't one for practical joking, but I still hoped he'd whip my boots out from under a bush, a wicked smile on his face.

Because the alternative was . . . well, that someone had taken them.

Or something . . .

Something that was hiding from us.

Chapter Forty-four

'I'm sorry to do this, Effie,' Dad said, 'but I've got
to make that meeting.'

'I don't mind, Dad,' I said. 'I really don't.'

'Well, it's not ideal, but Bill and Deidre are at
the hospital seeing to her.'

That morning Dad had woken me.

'It's Rosemary,' he said. 'She had a fall by the
loch last night and has gone into hospital. I've a
meeting I can't get out of. There's no one to mind
Tommi.'

'I'll do it,' I volunteered immediately.

'You've got school.'

'I'll catch up,' I said. 'Finn'll help me.
Honestly – it's fine, Dad.'

He kept apologizing all the way out of the
door. He used to let me stay off school quite often –
until Miss Bell had spoken to him about the
amount I was missing. Now he rarely let me miss a
day and begged the other oldies to take Tommi if

one of them couldn't make it. But today they were all occupied with Rosemary Tanner.

'I'll be home by six,' Dad said. 'I'll ring Miss Bell and ask her to send some work home with Finn.'

I groaned inwardly at the thought, but waved him out.

'Right, Tommi, it's just you and me,' I said, but Tommi was busy playing with the smooth oval pebbles she'd laid out on the floor and didn't look up.

I rang Finn to tell him I wouldn't be coming in and not to hold the bus for me. I washed up the breakfast things, collected our dirty laundry and filled the washing machine. I played with Tommi for a bit, but she was still more interested in her pebbles, and so I found myself in the unusual position of not having anything to do.

I decided to work on my map of Mivtown. I had been neglecting it recently, what with everything that had happened, and so I brought it down to the kitchen table and unrolled it carefully, securing the corners with anything I could find – a banana, a set of keys, a discarded fork.

The last time I worked on it, I had drawn in the places that Mum liked to visit. Now I added another little mark, a small x, just by Rosemary Tanner's cottage and close to the loch. This was where she said she'd seen Mum at seven that morning; after that, she'd never been seen again. It was the last place she'd been before disappearing for ever.

'Let's go out,' I said to Tommi, rolling up my map. 'Let's go for a walk.'

I bundled us both up in coats, gloves, hats and scarves; we looked like overstuffed snowmen as we stomped towards the loch.

Tommi ran ahead of me through the village, but I called her back when we neared Rosemary Tanner's cottage.

'Stay next to me, Tommi. Come here,' I shouted to her, and remembered Old Bill's reasoning that the legend was about keeping children away from the deep waters of the loch. It looked grey and solid in the distance, as though you could walk on it.

'Tommi! Come back!' I shouted a little louder, and something in my voice reminded me of Mum on the night of the Tindlemas, calling me over to her, insisting that we hold hands the whole way round the loch. Tommi looped back to me and I held her mitten securely in my own, as Mum had held mine all those months ago.

'Good girl,' I said. 'Let's stay together for this bit.'

Our breath curled into smoke in the cold

winter air. I pointed this out to Tommi, and she was fascinated by it, and huffed and puffed all the more.

'You wee dragon,' I said, laughing at her. Because I was looking at Tommi, I didn't notice them straight away.

It was the oldies. I could see them clearly through the little window of the cottage: Old Bill, Mr and Mrs Daniels, and Rosemary Tanner herself. Not in the hospital in Abiemore at all, but standing together in the living room of the stone cottage.

Chapter Forty-five

'Over here, Tommi,' I said, and quickly pulled her behind the wall that ran along the path and up to the cottage, out of sight.

'Hold onto my hand, Tommi, and no talking, OK? As quiet as we can. We're going to tiptoe because . . . because . . .'

Tommi looked up at me expectantly.

'We are stepping on a sleeping giant and we don't want to wake him. OK? Really quiet.'

Tommi's eyes widened, and she looked down at the grass as though to check on the giant. When she looked back at me, she closed her mouth firmly so her cheeks puffed out a little. We started to tiptoe.

'That's it,' I whispered. 'Just like that. Really quiet. We don't want to wake him.'

I was determined to get closer to the cottage and find out why the oldies had lied about Rosemary Tanner being in hospital. Why would they make up a story like that? And what was really stopping them from looking after Tommi today?

'This way, Tommi.' I gestured for her to follow me. 'Quietly!' We crept along the wall towards the cottage – although I wasn't sure if we would hear anything as the windows were shut, the stone walls thick and solid.

All at once I heard the door open, and then heavy footsteps – Old Bill. Then came the lighter steps of Mrs Daniels, with Mr Daniels following after. The door closed behind them with a slam.

I mimed at Tommi to keep quiet, and she nodded at me in agreement and put a finger to her lips, a mirror of me. I squeezed her mitten and we stood there, unmoving; for a moment it was as if we were part of the wall itself.

At first the oldies didn't speak, and I thought they were going to leave the cottage and we would learn nothing more than we knew already.

Then I heard Old Bill clear his throat.

'She's not in a good way, is she?' he said gruffly.

There was no answer, and I imagined Mr and Mrs Daniels shaking their heads in agreement. I kept as still as I could, but Tommi was tugging at my hand. She wanted to pick up something on the ground, and as she knelt down, she made a rustling noise – which was masked by Mrs Daniels's voice:

'She's terrible. Just terrible. What a state she's in.'

They were walking away now.

'We'll pop back in an hour or so – do you want to come back a bit later?' Mrs Daniels asked.

Their footsteps carried on along the path, their voices becoming faint. I was beginning to think that Rosemary Tanner had fallen after all, and that they had just come back from the hospital – but then a phrase sailed through the air to me like an arrow released from a bow.

'. . . can't stop talking about those slugs . . .' Mr Daniels said, and then their voices receded until I couldn't make out a word of what they were saying.

Chapter Forty-six

Everyone knows that if you visit someone who is sick or has had bad news, you have to bring them something. When Mum disappeared, people kept bringing us food and flowers – so many that we ran out of vases and jugs and had to make do with jam jars and tin cans.

I cast around the undergrowth for something to pick for Mrs Tanner, but as it was winter, there was not a lot to choose from.

'Come on, Tommi,' I said as we made our way past the cottage, ducking under the window and looking around.

That was when I saw it. The bladderwort. I was sure it wasn't the right time of year for it to flower, but the dainty yellow heads nodded at me gaily in the breeze; the whole area looked like a mossy green and yellow blur.

I picked a few hurriedly, remembering that Mrs Daniels had said she was going to return, and when I had something resembling a bunch, I took Tommi's hand and said to her, 'Let's go and see Rosemary Tanner. She's sick.'

I suspected that Rosemary Tanner knew more about the slugs that she had let on, and after Mrs Daniels mentioned them, I was convinced of it.

'R'mary Tanner,' echoed Tommi. 'Sick.'

'That's right,' I said.

I knocked three times with the black iron knocker, but there was no answer, so I pushed open the letter box and called through.

'It's Effie and Tommi come to see you,' I said. 'We've brought you something.'

I heard movement inside the cottage, and sure enough, the door swung open and Rosemary Tanner stood in front of us.

I had expected her to look ill, to be wearing a dressing gown, but not a hair of her stiff grey bun was out of place, and her eyes were flooded with an energy I had not seen before. She was wearing her usual tweed suit and she smiled at us, showing all her yellowed teeth.

'Come in, come in, wee Tommi, Effie.'

I hesitated, doubting the decision that had brought us there.

'Out of the cold, the pair of you,' Rosemary

Tanner commanded, and I found my legs moving forward as though I were a robot.

'We heard you weren't well and so we brought you something,' I said, and offered the wilting flowers.

Rosemary Tanner looked at the bladderwort with barely disguised disgust, but took the bunch off to the kitchen. 'Who told you that I wasn't well?' she asked.

'Dad. He said you'd had a fall and the old— I mean, everyone was with you. Did you just get back from the hospital?'

'Hmm,' Rosemary Tanner said, not answering. 'So that's what they're saying, is it. Anyway, you two must be freezing. Cup of tea? I've got a fruitcake that needs eating.'

'Oh, we just ate,' I said quickly. 'We can't stay long. Just wanted to see how you were. And say sorry about your fall.'

'Nonsense,' she replied. 'You'll both stay for a slice, now you're here. Sit down.' She reminded me of Miss Bell.

I sat in a high-backed chair covered in faded material patterned with flying birds, and pulled Tommi onto my lap. I'd never been inside the cottage before, and the more I looked around the walls, the more I noticed. There were watercolours of Mivtown – mostly of the loch, black and brooding, more like a bottomless hole than a stretch of water. And there were lots of porcelain birds, as well as feathers tucked into vases, and even a tiny nest containing three impossibly small speckled eggs.

'Here we are,' Rosemary Tanner said, and set down a tray complete with teapot and cups and three slices of fruitcake studded with raisins and gleaming red cherries that looked like jewels.

'Erm – thank you, Mrs Tanner. So, are you feeling better?' I looked at her closely, but she ignored my question.

'Any more slugs?' she asked.

'Er . . . a few – you know,' I answered.

'You know what is happening, don't you? You feel it too, like I do. I'm right, aren't I?'

Rosemary Tanner fixed me with one of her hungry, fierce looks and carried on talking – although she now seemed to be somewhere far away from us.

'It's the legend,' she continued. 'I told you they would come. I did, I did. As soon as . . . I did. Ever since, ever since . . . I told you, I told you. The girl born after a boy—'

Suddenly she stopped and looked around anxiously, as though she didn't know where she was or who she was talking to.

231

'I think we'd better be going,' I said quickly, standing up and holding Tommi tightly.

'No, no, no.' Rosemary Tanner shook her head.

'We've got to get back,' I said, more firmly.

'Don't you want a cup of tea?' She leaned forward to pour the tea into the delicate little teacups. The teapot looked heavy, and she had to grip the handle tightly to lift it, her hand trembling with the weight – and that was when I noticed it.

It was the black notebook, the one she always carried around with her: on the open page I saw a shadowy drawing that was, unmistakably, a slug.

The first drop of blood was dark, almost black. It looked like a tear. It made me think of the last time I let myself cry. The day Da passed. I told myself that nothing would be worse, that I would never let myself cry over anything else because it would be trivial in comparison.

Then came the day at the loch.

I shouldn't have left her there.

They are coming for me now.

Chapter Forty-seven

Later that day, when Dad was back with Tommi, Finn asked me why I hadn't asked Rosemary Tanner about the legend.

'I just felt uneasy there. She seemed like she was – I don't know, not really there. It was like she thought she was talking to a different person. And then I saw the picture of the slug in her notebook and I just had to leave.'

When I saw it, I got up and just blurted out, 'Sorry, sorry, sorry,' like a siren, and we'd left without giving Rosemary Tanner time to see us out. Without even looking back.

'It was all so weird, Finn,' I said. 'It was like she hadn't had a fall at all; she seemed just like normal – or maybe a little weirder than usual. But she hadn't hurt herself, she was walking fine. And yet the oldies were definitely worried about her: they were planning when to come and check on her throughout the day. And then the bladderwort!'

'What about it?'

'It was flowering.'

'But that flowers in June at the earliest!'

'And there was loads of it, Finn. All in this little spot by the loch.'

Finn scratched his head.

'I picked some,' I continued, 'to give to her. But I don't think she liked it.'

'Did she ask where you got it from?'

'No. But I could tell she didn't like it.'

'I think we should go back and see Rosemary Tanner. Together,' he said. 'She might tell us more if we're both there, without Tommi. Shall we go now? We could check on the raft too if we've got time.' We still wanted to see whether it floated all right, before we did any more to it.

'We might bump into Old Bill or Mr and Mrs Daniels,' I warned Finn. 'I think they are going in to see her every hour or so.'

As we approached the cottage, we saw a few lights; they illuminated the semi-darkness around us – night was creeping steadily, stealthily towards us.

I reached for the knocker, but as I did so, the door swung open by itself.

'Hello?' Finn called out. 'It's Finn. And Effie. Hello?'

'She's not there,' I said, sensing the stillness within.

'Let's have a quick look around.'

'Finn!' I hissed, but he had already disappeared into the cottage. I followed him in.

The small living room was exactly as I had left it earlier, right down to the cups of tea sitting on the table, their contents now grey and filmy. The only difference was the black notebook: it had been lying with its pages open; now it was face down on the table, as though someone had just put it to rest for a moment while something else distracted them.

I walked towards it and turned it over.

I knew almost immediately that it was something I should not be reading. Here and there the writing was small and cramped, the letters squashed into one another; in other places it was looping and large and filled the page. But I knew intuitively that the person who had written those words had wanted to keep them private. It wasn't about village life at all.

'Finn!' I said. 'I've found the notebook.'

'What does it say?' he asked.

'It's not about the village; it's a . . . it's a diary. There's dates, but it's hard to read.'

As I flicked through, something fluttered from in between the pages.

Finn picked it up and looked at it closely before handing it to me. 'It's her, isn't it?'

I put down the notebook and took it. It was a very old photograph. Two children holding hands – a brother and sister, perhaps, though they were so close in size, I immediately wondered if they were twins. The girl, as Finn had thought, reminded me of Rosemary Tanner, although she looked as if she were about to burst into laughter – an expression I had never seen on the Mrs Tanner I knew.

'Effie, you'd better see this,' Finn said. He was flicking through the diary and had stopped at one page, pointing to a word.

'What is it?' I asked.

Then I saw it.

The word he was pointing to. A word that was scattered across the page.

Tori.

Tori walked right up to me this morning. Right into the space that I inhabit. That was her first mistake. But the second was mine.

I can't remember what it was she was talking about – something about the girl – but I do remember how angry she was. Her nostrils flared like a horse's, I remember thinking. A panting horse. Her eyes were wide. Furious.

She was too close. Much too close, and so I did exactly what Da taught me to do if someone got in my way.

I pushed.

Chapter Forty-eight

'*I pushed,*' I read aloud.

My voice stumbled over the words, but I read on.

'*Tori fell back towards the bank. Stumbled, really. As if she had tripped on the path. Her legs gave way beneath her like broken sticks. Then I heard a sound I shouldn't have. A dull crack. A heavy thud. Something breaking, hard.*

'*I didn't need to look to know that there was . . . there was . . . stone where her head fell. She just lay there. Unmoving. Almost as though she were resting.*

'*I turned round and walked away; it seemed like the easiest thing to do. By the time I reached my door it was like nothing untoward had happened that morning.*'

I dropped the diary and it fell to the floor with a heavy thud.

'Rosemary Tanner . . .' Finn said. 'She knew all along.'

I thought of Mum. Falling on the ground. Lying in a heap. And Rosemary Tanner turning her back on her and walking away. Did she die then? The moment when she fell? Or was she hanging on, hoping for help? Waiting for someone to find her?

'What did Rosemary Tanner do to her? Why couldn't we find her?'

'There's more,' Finn said, having picked up the diary. 'She goes back a little while later, but your mum's disappeared. There's no trace of her.'

'How could that be?' I said, my voice wobbling.

'She thinks . . . she thinks . . . it has something to do with the monsters. They have taken her into the loch.'

From the small rectangular window in Rosemary Tanner's sitting room, you can see part of the loch. The middle, where it is deepest. It looked grey. Still, like a stone, and hard, not like water at all.

'We have to find Rosemary Tanner,' I said. My mind was racing, unable to keep up with everything it was hearing, but I could only see the figure of Rosemary Tanner, her hawkish stance, the eyes that had always unnerved me.

'Let's try the loch,' Finn said, and we ran away from the cottage and the diary and the cold cups of tea set out so neatly on the table.

Chapter Forty-nine

'There she is,' Finn said, before I'd seen her.

Rosemary Tanner was just by the flowering bladderwort.

And she was wading into the loch.

'What's she—' Finn started to say, but then he broke into a run towards her.

'Mrs Tanner! Rosemary!' he shouted. 'Come out! Turn back!'

We ran to the water's edge, calling so loudly that surely everyone in the village would hear us.

But she did not stop; it was as though she were in a trance or under some kind of spell. Her ears were deaf to our shouts.

She waded in, deeper and deeper. It seemed to happen very slowly, but then with every step, a little more of her disappeared under the water. Darkness had started to fall, and it seemed as if she was becoming part of it, absorbed into it.

'We've got to get her back, Effie – she'll drown,' Finn said.

'But . . . but . . .' I said.

'I'll wade in.' Finn took a step into the icy water. He shivered at its touch. 'You get the raft. The Tree Cave's not far away.'

I didn't want us to be parted. 'Don't go too far in. I'll be right back.'

In the fading light I darted off through the trees, following the path I knew so well that I could find my way even in the gloom. The raft was where we had left it, carefully tucked under a tarpaulin. I pulled the cover off roughly and lifted it onto its side so that I could drag it. I tucked the paddle under my arm and started to haul the raft back down the path towards the loch.

It was heavier than it looked. I strained to pull it through the trees, and only the thought of my Finn wading into the icy water to save Rosemary Tanner gave me the strength to keep going.

When I reached the loch at last, the water looked peaceful and black. The sky had become its dark mirror as the night drew in around me.

There was no sign of Rosemary Tanner.

And there was no sign of Finn.

Chapter Fifty

'Finn!' I shouted – so loudly that it echoed around the loch in answer to itself.

'Finn!' I cried desperately. I pushed the raft into the loch and threw myself on it. It wobbled and bucked, but righted itself quickly, and I began to paddle out into the black water.

'Finn! Finn! Finn!'

By the light of the moon I thought I saw a bobbing head, and paddled as hard as I could towards it, making my own waves all around me. Desperate splashes replaced the sound of my shouts.

But when I got to the place where I had glimpsed it, there was nothing there; the water all started to look the same. I could no longer tell where Rosemary Tanner had been heading, each ripple and wave part of the same repeating pattern.

I thought of the flowering bladderwort; looking over to the water's edge, I saw the patch of yellow where the flowers clustered. That was where

Rosemary Tanner and then Finn had entered the water. I quickly paddled round to line myself up with the flowers, and then, without looking at the glossy surface of the black water, I jumped in.

The cold stabbed into me like a thousand needles, paralysing my arms and legs. I felt myself begin to sink, a heavy lead weight, and desperately kicked upwards, my arms flailing, reaching.

I broke the surface and saw for just a moment the round, glinting circle of the white moon and the shadow of our raft bobbing on the surface. Filling my lungs until they felt as if they might burst, I sank back down in search of Finn, in search of Rosemary Tanner.

I kicked out desperately, and was sure that my foot had touched something, or that something had touched it. My eyes were tightly closed, though even if they'd been open, I would not have been able to see, so I simply explored all around me with my hands.

That was when I felt it.

Its skin was cold and as slippery as the body of a slug. It slid away, and I felt the strength and power within it as it surged past, making whirlpools around me.

I was not alone in the water.

Chapter Fifty-one

As I hung there, as motionless as the bladderwort that also made its home in the loch, I thought of Finn. We had been led into the water, as the legend had foretold, and only if we fought and struggled against its power would we escape it.

The thought propelled me to life and I reached out for Finn's hand, a part of his trousers or coat. He had to be down there too.

The chill of the water had penetrated my bones, and there was a part of me that, more than anything, wanted to stop struggling and just be; to become part of the water, another ripple upon its surface, a drop in the pool. And then I thought of Finn again, and I kicked out and beat my arms around me as though trying to escape from something.

I thought of Mum too. Had she done this? Had she kicked out and fought, and then let it roll over her like a mist as the biting cold immobilized her?

I knew that I didn't have long to find them. I kept thinking of the powerful monster that had swept past me with the grace of a serpent. Were there others? Would their mouths rasp my skin and mark me with my own blood as the slugs had done?

I kicked up to the surface once more and drew the air deep into my lungs. I thought I saw a figure on the path by the loch, a shadow by the trees, but I didn't have time to linger before I began to sink down again.

Finn! Finn! I shouted with my mind. *Finn!* I clawed my way out into the darkness as though I were in a fight, and immediately felt something in the water. Not the silky, ancient skin of a creature, but the texture of fabric.

It made me think of the material of Mum's dress, the one patterned with bladderwort, worn and soft. This was far rougher, thicker, heavier. I reached out for it once more, but this time I held it fast in my fist. I kicked upwards, awkwardly and desperately, for what I held onto hung in the water like a dead weight.

I felt it slip between my fingers, and so I grabbed hold with my other hand too as I tugged it up with me.

Please let it be Finn. Please let it be Finn.

I pulled it up and up – until at last my head broke the surface and I saw the blurry circle of the moon overhead.

'Finn! Finn!' I shouted to the body in my arms.

I had him. I held him.

His skin looked even paler than the moon and he did not answer me.

Chapter Fifty-two

I kicked towards the raft, which sat bobbing on the ripples, and tried to swing Finn up onto the deck; he was too heavy to lift and I could only rest his head on the platform. I held onto him, my arms wrapped around him, sure that if I let go, we would begin to sink under the water. The very thought made me grip him tighter still. My fingers felt like claws, numb from being clamped onto the edge of the raft.

And so I started our painful journey back to shore.

With every kick I thought of Rosemary Tanner disappearing into the blackness, and of the powerful body that had swept past me under the water, but I couldn't let go of Finn, not for a moment. I told myself that I would go back and find her once Finn was safely ashore. There was a voice needling me, reminding me that Rosemary Tanner had left my mum, that she hadn't gone back for her, but there was a louder one telling me that I was not like her, that I could be different.

I pushed and kicked the raft back towards the shore. I barely seemed to be moving at all, and I was already exhausted. Soon I felt myself sinking, and Finn slipping away from me. I couldn't hold onto him and propel the raft forward at the same time.

Finn felt impossibly heavy now, like a feeling that overwhelms you. I knew I didn't have the strength to pull him back onto the raft, or to drag him to shore. I chose to hold onto him.

We started to sink.

For one moment something became so clear to me that it seemed to be happening in front of my eyes; not like imagining at all. I thought: *This is how they will find us, locked together, my arms around Finn in a never-ending clasp.*

I shut my eyes as I felt the cold water surround me. Despite the ache in my chest and limbs, I kept my arms tightly around Finn. We were sinking deeper. The freezing water paralysed me.

All I could do was hold onto Finn. It took every last bit of energy, and I knew that clinging onto him would be the last thing I ever did.

Then something moved beneath us. I felt a nudge against my foot. The touch of something solid.

For a horrible moment I thought that we had reached the bottom of the loch; we'd sunk so far that we could go no further.

But then, all at once, there was a great surge of water beneath us; a wave that lifted us, a huge movement that swept the dark water, and us with it, towards the surface.

It drove us upwards. We rose up through the loch, and then, just as we began to sink once more, it came again. Like the sweep of a tail, it propelled us on.

We surged forward with its beat, and I felt my head break the water's surface and heard my ragged, broken gasp before we sank down once more and my ears filled with the muffled silence.

And again it came, and again and again. Insistently. Mighty and strong. A strange pulsing movement from underneath that carried us through the water.

Then strong arms were pulling us up, and I felt Finn being taken from me.

'We've got you.'

'You're all right.'

'We're here.'

Voices I knew as well as my own. Dad's and Rob's and Old Bill's. But there were also sobs and cries.

I looked over to see Finn's lifeless face: he'd been laid out on the ground on his side. Then Kathleen and Rob leaned over him and I couldn't see him any more, and my mind went blank and I felt my body fall in on itself and collapse beneath me.

Chapter Fifty-three

'Easy does it, Effie.'

I heard his voice before I saw his face. Dad.

'Finn,' I spluttered. 'Finn.'

My throat felt raw and my voice was hoarse.

'He's all right, he's all right. He wouldn't have been, without you, but he's all right. Rob got him breathing again – he still needs warming up, but he's OK. He's going to be fine.'

I looked around at the strange green and white room. The sharp, sweet scent of disinfectant hung in the air. It was not exactly unpleasant, but like the stiff, smooth sheets of the bed I was lying in, it felt unfamiliar, strange.

'Where are we?'

'Abiemore. At the hospital.' Dad bent over the bed and gently tucked my hair behind my ear, just as Mum used to do when I was little and she'd read me a story and I was about to fall asleep.

His eyes were red. 'I could have lost you. Effie,

I could have lost you. I'm sorry I haven't been . . . I haven't been . . . there. For you. I'm so sorry, Eff—' His voice cracked and he looked away from me, his eyes filling with tears.

'It's OK, Dad, it's OK.' I tried to reach out to him but found that my arm was too heavy.

Dad took my hand and laid it down at my side, holding it carefully. He didn't let go. 'Things will be different, I promise,' he continued. 'I've been expecting too much of you. I've spoken to Kathleen and Rob, and we're all agreed: things will be better now, I promise. For all of us. You, me and Tommi.'

'Rosemary Tanner,' I said in a whisper, although I already knew the answer.

Dad gave a tiny shake of his head in answer.

'Dad, I have to tell you something—' I started to say, but Dad cut me off.

'It's OK,' he said. 'Rosemary had not been very well. In her head. You two did everything you could. You did. We are so proud of you – of what you did to try and save her.'

'But . . . but it's more than that, Dad. We found out stuff about Mum. And the loch. There was something in the water,' I said in alarm, remembering. 'It wasn't just us – the monsters . . .'

'Shush, shush now,' Dad said. 'Don't go upsetting yourself, my love.'

'But Dad – but Dad . . .' I said desperately, wanting to be heard.

At that point a nurse came in and Dad spoke to her and she came over to my bed. 'Easy – easy there.' She stroked my arm and said in a soothing voice, 'Deep breaths now, Effie – that's it, in and out. Try not to speak, concentrate on your breathing.'

She rang for a doctor, who checked me over, and then, when they both seemed satisfied, I was left alone with Dad again.

'Would you like to see Finn?' he asked me before I could say any more.

'Can I?' I said excitedly.

'As long as you take it easy and stay calm,' he said. 'There's a wheelchair here we can use.'

'I don't think I'll need it,' I said, but I couldn't walk properly; it was like my legs were made of rubber and had forgotten that they belonged to me, so Dad lifted me into the wheelchair and pushed me all the way to Finn's room.

'Effie!' Kathleen and Rob held me close. 'Thank you, dear girl. Thank you for saving him,' Kathleen whispered into my ear.

'Is he going to be OK?' I said. He wasn't awake and he lay very, very still.

'The doctors say he's going to be just fine,'

Rob said. 'He woke up just a little while ago. He was asking for you.'

'Can I touch him?' I asked.

'Of course, love,' Kathleen said, and Dad wheeled my chair over so I could reach up for his hand.

It felt warm, full of life, and I squeezed it.

I was sure I felt a tiny squeeze back, but he was still sleeping, so I must have imagined it.

Chapter Fifty-four

We stayed in hospital for a few more days. 'Just to be on the safe side.' My doctor had straight brown hair that she pushed behind her ears and a smile that made me think of Mum.

Dad and Tommi came in to see me every day. As did Kathleen and Rob. They would all come together.

'She misses you,' Dad said as Tommi hugged me tightly. He had to tell her to 'Be gentle with Effie – she's still mending, you know.'

I did feel like I was mending. Almost as if bits and pieces of me were being put in their right places again, and day by day I was beginning to feel whole.

Finn and I hung out in each other's rooms so much that in the end the nurses relented and put us in one together; then they no longer had to keep chasing one of us out.

We spoke about our memories of what had

happened. Finn's are much patchier than mine. He barely remembers anything after trying to dive in after Rosemary Tanner's head had disappeared under the water.

We also talked about discovering the diary, what we had found out about Mum and how we were going to tell our families . . . It was a strange time, and I often started crying without realizing it. It was as if something had left me – a weight and a feeling, something like a memory, all mixed up together. I felt very raw, very fragile, and when I remembered what we had discovered, that Mum had died by the loch that day, I thought I might crumple in on myself, collapse.

I opened my mouth to speak the words, but each time I found I couldn't, that the words were getting stuck in my throat; I couldn't force them out, however hard I tried.

It was easier to talk about the monster.

'Did you feel anything else in the water with us?' I asked Finn. 'Did you see anything else?'

But I was the only one who'd felt the monster, and I told him all about it. The way it had dived down; the size of it. The feeling as it gently nudged me, pushing me towards the shore when I was sinking. We wondered how that could be and why it had helped us.

And then we had a visit from Old Bill.

He looked too big to fit into the small plastic hospital chairs, and had to scrunch up his body in order to sit down.

'I didn't want to come when your folks were here,' he said, and he took off his hat but then didn't know where to put it; he ended up balancing it awkwardly on his knee.

'How are you both?' he said, but I noticed that he didn't look us in the eye when he spoke. He was gazing intently at the floor.

'The doctor said we can come home soon,' I said.

'I've got a couple more tests,' Finn added.

'Good, good,' Old Bill said, although I don't think he had heard what we said.

He started to say something, but then shook his head, as though disagreeing with someone.

'I've come to tell you something. I thought you had the right to know first.'

We looked at him expectantly.

'We found something. In Rosemary's cottage.'

Old Bill paused and suddenly rubbed one eye. I noticed how tired he looked. His shoulders sagged as if he were carrying something – a weight, a secret, something we could not see.

'I've just come from there. It explains a lot

and I think you deserve to know the truth. They're talking about burying it, burning it, pretending it doesn't exist, and so what I'm about to tell you – there may no longer be any evidence of it. And I don't think the others will support you.'

'Rosemary Tanner's diary?' I managed to say.

'You know about that?' Old Bill swallowed hard.

'We found it. Just before we saw her in the loch.'

'Did you read it?'

'Only some of it,' Finn said. 'The part about Effie's mum. We know what happened. Well, of course we don't really. We don't understand how she disappeared – after Rosemary Tanner pushed her.'

The air was very still, as though time itself were hanging onto the last second by the thread of a spider's web.

'I'm very sorry,' Old Bill said. 'I had no idea that she was involved.'

'What I don't understand,' I said, my voice sounding stronger than I felt, 'is why she did it. You knew something was wrong, didn't you? I heard you talking on the phone. It was to Rosemary Tanner, wasn't it?'

'I knew that Rosemary was not very well. She was going over the same things in her head, over and over. I thought it was just in her head. It started so long ago: when you were born, just after Finn, Rosemary thought that the prophecy was coming true.'

'But you said *twins*,' Finn said.

'Well, that's how I saw it, and many others did too, but when the pair of you were born – on the same day, a girl after a boy – Rosemary thought the legend was coming true. She said you were as close as twins could be. You've always been inseparable, even when you were bairns. Never wanted to be parted, so I heard. Rosemary saw how attached you were.'

I thought, a little grimly, of the conversation I'd overheard the night we went to Finn's house about how I'd behaved when I was younger.

'So she thought you, Effie, would awaken the monsters. She had monsters in her head, did Rosemary. She didn't think she was making it up. She was the one, you see – she was the one who had made the curse in the first place. It all started with her.'

'She was the twin from the story?'

'That's right. Rosemary and Robert. They were inseparable. Like you two.' Old Bill closed his eyes for a moment, then suddenly put his hand to his chest as though there was a pain there.

He breathed in deeply and began again. 'I was there – I saw it happen. We were daring each other, as young 'uns do; daring each other to swim out into the loch. Our parents had told us about the monsters – that story is as old as the land – but Rosemary, she was fearless. She went into the water anyway. She went so far out that we could barely see her from the shore; she was just the smallest of dots. Robert kept his eyes on her like a hawk. He saw it first – the moment she disappeared under the water. He dived in, and swam and swam to the spot where she had gone under, while Deidre went to get help from the village. Their pa came running up. He was frantic, and dived straight in and swam out to them, but when he got there, he could only find Rosemary. She was babbling when he pulled out. There was something in the water, she said, something that had dragged Robert away. The monsters of the loch. She described their cold, slimy skin; she had felt it brush past her arms. No one believed her, not really. We thought it was just something she'd imagined to help her cope with Robert's death. But she didn't let it go. She said she'd started the curse. She had led Robert into the water, it had been her. *The girl twin. The girl born after the boy.* And she made us play along with the legend – the offerings, Tindlemas . . . It was her way of coping.

Anyway, when you two came along, she told your ma, Effie, that she thought you would awaken the monsters, that you needed to be stopped. I suppose your ma felt protective – she didn't know how far Rosemary would go. She didn't . . . trust her, I suppose.

'Your ma went to confront her that morning – it was something Rosemary had said about that rabbit of yours . . .'

'Buster! What about him?'

'Seems like Rosemary had let him out of his cage. As part of the offering. Your ma had worked it out. She spoke to Rosemary about it, and – and . . . that's when it happened. The accident. I don't think Rosemary meant to hurt her, but you know that part of the story.'

'But why didn't we find her?' I cried out. 'Where was she?'

Old Bill's face wrinkled with sadness. 'I don't know. The diary says—'

'We read that part,' Finn said. 'She thought Effie's mum had been taken by the monsters. Do you believe that?'

'I don't know what I believe any more.'

We sat there, the three of us, letting Old Bill's

words settle around us like snowflakes, weaving together to make a blanket of snow.

'I'm sorry,' he said. 'You'll want to tell your dad about it . . . You should. Or I can, if you want me to. I don't know what will happen – if they will destroy the diary or not. I tried to stop them, talk them out of it, but although they loved your mum, they're trying to protect Rosemary the only way they know how. It's not the right way to go about it, but people don't see things clearly when they are grieving. They're holding onto something. Rosemary wasn't found, you see. They didn't find her body.'

'I don't know if anyone will believe us,' I said honestly.

'I'll tell the truth,' Old Bill said.

'Can I ask you something?' Finn said. 'Did Mrs Tanner write about the monsters during the last few weeks?'

'She wrote about nothing else. She thought they were coming for her because of what she'd done to Tori. She believed that they would lead her into the water.' Old Bill sat up straight, as though a thought had just occurred to him. 'It was as if she believed it so much that she made it true.'

Epilogue

There is a little spot by the loch of Mivtown where, whatever the season when you happen to pass by, yellow clusters of bladderwort can be seen.

Finn and I believe that this was where my mum died. We've marked it in the only way we know how: with a collection of stones, pebbles and feathers. We take Tommi there all the time, although we still shy away from the water, the memories of sinking never far from our minds.

One day, not long after we left hospital, we sat Dad, Kathleen and Rob down and – along with Old Bill – told them about Mrs Tanner's diary. The oldies didn't destroy it in the end, and so they could read the whole thing for themselves, but Finn and I told them how we had discovered it that day, just before we spotted Mrs Tanner by the loch.

I found my words again. 'Mum didn't leave us,' I told Dad.

She didn't leave us, he kept saying, over and over again. *She didn't leave us. She didn't leave us.*

He held my hand tightly, as though he were never going to let it go.

They all cried when we told them, and tears streamed down my cheeks too, but I didn't wipe them away. Like Mum: she used to let them collect on her chin and drop onto her lap.

Not long afterwards, everyone in the village agreed that the loch should be searched again. This time we found Rosemary Tanner.

And we found Mum.

We had another funeral, but I no longer worried about how to behave, and afterwards we all walked to the bladderwort spot. We shared stories, remembering things we had forgotten or had not spoken of in a long time.

'Remember when your mum went cartwheeling down the hill?' Kathleen said.

'I remember that!' Finn said. 'I thought she might start flying!'

'She was very proud when you did your first one, Effie,' Dad said. 'Do you remember? You were out in the garden, practising over and over, and your mum was watching you from the kitchen. I heard a shriek. *She did it!* She yelled so loudly that I almost dropped my drink!'

'She always used to pick a little bunch of wild flowers when it was my birthday, or Dad's, or Tommi's. She put it next to our breakfast plate,' I said. 'I'm going to keep doing it for Tommi when it's her birthday.'

'Oh, she did love the three of you,' Kathleen said, and for a little while no one spoke.

We never had a slug in the house again. After the day in the loch they just stopped coming. Finn and I can't explain it fully, but maybe they were sort of messengers sent to us by the monsters; they were trying to tell us what had happened to Mum. That's why they came to the house and covered things that meant a lot to her – Buster's grave, her binoculars. They were sending us a message. Not bad creatures, after all.

I still have a small scar where I was bitten. It looks like a freckle. I remember how it shocked me at the time, but it didn't really hurt. It was just a prick. 'Like they were trying to get our attention,' Finn mused.

We never saw anything in the loch again. Sometimes I think that if I look long enough or hard enough, I might see the monsters, but it hasn't happened yet, and I know in my heart that it won't.

I see Kathleen, Rob and Finn a lot, although I no longer wish for a different place in a different family.

I feel lucky for all the people in my life – Dad, Tommi, Finn, Kathleen, Rob, Old Bill – connected to me by blood, or love, by friendship or sadness; it makes for a glorious map. We are interconnected and find new places amongst us every day.

Sometimes I find myself thinking of my last night with Mum. It feels prickly in my mind, like I can't quite hold it or touch it. Finn says that I have to forgive myself. At first I didn't understand how to do that – until Dad said it was about knowing that you would have liked to do something differently but understanding that you can't now because it's in the past. I said something cruel that night and I wish I hadn't. I know I can't change that; the moment is behind me now. That's OK.

I've found that I miss Mum more, not less, as time passes and the gap since I last saw her widens and deepens.

I think of her often. And I want her back.

But I see her in the ripples in the loch.

And feel her love in the clusters of yellow flowers that wave to me in the wind.

ACKNOWLEDGEMENTS

My thanks to . . .

Clare Wallace, officially the best agent in existence. My very special thanks to you, you supremely talented, oh so lovely person. I'm hugely glad my books give us an excuse to hang out.

The wonderful Darley Anderson crew, especially Mary Darby and Emma Winter.

Kelly Hurst and Carmen McCullough, the duo of editing dreams who read, re-read, made suggestions, had better ideas than me, read again and came up with even better ideas. Also to Mainga Bhima, who joined us when we needed another pair of eyes.

The fantastic team at Penguin Random House Children's, particularly Dominica Clements, Jasmine Joynson, Tineke Mollemans, Eliza Walsh and Sophie Nelson.

My dad, for having read the book in its very first stirrings, then staying with it while it morphed completely and finally settled into the story it is today, and for emailing, 'Keep going, Pol,' throughout.

And finally, to Dan, who has not only made yet another stunning, stunning cover but who stayed up until 2 a.m. with me – on a school night, I hasten to add – covering our living-room floor with plot plans, questions and assorted-sized arrows, and remaining patient, funny and brilliant throughout. The thing is, he's patient, funny and brilliant every day. I believe I owe you a lifetime supply of Snickers now. Do see me about those.